DOVER·THRIFT·EDITIONS

The Oresteia Trilogy
Agamemnon, The Libation-Bearers and The Furies

AESCHYLUS

Translated by E. D. A. Morshead

DOVER PUBLICATIONS, INC.
Mineola, New York

DOVER THRIFT EDITIONS

GENERAL EDITOR: STANLEY APPELBAUM
EDITOR OF THIS VOLUME: ALAN WEISSMAN

Performance

This Dover Thrift Edition may be used in its entirety, in adaptation or in any other way for theatrical productions and performances, professional and amateur, in the United States, without fee, permission or acknowledgment. (This may not apply outside of the United States, as copyright conditions may vary.)

Copyright

Copyright ©1996 by Dover Publications, Inc.
All rights reserved under Pan American and International Copyright Conventions.

Published in Canada by General Publishing Company, Ltd., 30 Lesmill Road, Don Mills, Toronto, Ontario.
Published in the United Kingdom by Constable and Company, Ltd., 3 The Lanchesters, 162–164 Fulham Palace Road, London W6 9ER.

Bibliographical Note

This Dover edition, first published in 1996, is an unabridged republication of the English translation by E. D. A. Morshead, as it appeared, under the title "The House of Atreus," in *Nine Greek Dramas by Æschylus, Sophocles, Euripides and Aristophanes* (Volume 8 of The Harvard Classics), first published by P. F. Collier & Son, New York, 1909. A new introductory Note has been specially prepared for this edition.

Library of Congress Cataloging-in-Publication Data

Aeschylus.
    [Oresteia. English]
    The Oresteia trilogy / translated by E.D.A. Morshead.
        p.   cm. — (Dover thrift editions)
    Republication of the English translation by E.D.A. Morshead under the title: "The House of Atreus" in "Nine Greek Dramas by Aeschylus, Sophocles, Euripides, and Aristophanes" (v. 8 of The Harvard classics), 1909.
    Contents: Agamemnon — The libation-bearers — The furies.
    ISBN 0-486-29242-8 (pbk.)
    1. Aeschylus — Translations into English.   2. Greek drama (Tragedy) — Translations into English.   3. Agamemnon (Greek mythology) — Drama.   4. Orestes (Greek mythology) — Drama.   5. Electra (Greek mythology) — Drama.   I. Aeschylus. Agamemnon. II. Aeschylus. Libation-bearers. III. Aeschylus. Furies. IV. Aeschylus. Selections. English. 1928.   V. Title.   VI. Title: Agamemnon. VII. Title: Libation-bearers. VIII. Title: Furies. IX. Series.
PA3827.A7M7   1996
883'.01 — dc20
                            96-13715
                                CIP

Manufactured in the United States of America
Dover Publications, Inc., 31 East 2nd Street, Mineola, N.Y. 11501

Note

If anyone may be said to have "invented" the kind of drama we know as Greek tragedy, it was Aeschylus (525–456/5 B.C.). The drama he wrote, like that of his predecessors, was derived from choral song and dance and played an important role in the religious and cultural life of the community. Yet, besides the chorus, only one actor appeared in a given scene in early Greek tragedy. Aeschylus' stroke of genius was to add a second actor, thereby vastly increasing the dramatic possibilities.

The next generation brought the great dramatists Sophocles and Euripides, who added further refinements. With the surviving plays of these three — and there are only 32 such plays — we have all the complete examples left to us of one of the greatest and most influential arts of Western civilization. Aeschylus' *Oresteia* is a trilogy — that is, three connected plays performed on the same day. Apart from its innate worth, this group of plays is notable as the only trilogy that has survived intact of all the Greek drama that has come down to us.

Like most Greek tragedy as we know it, the *Oresteia* is based on characters and situations of ancient Greek mythology, an intimate part of the cultural heritage of Aeschylus' contemporaries, and the audience of the *Agamemnon*, the first of the three plays, would have been well prepared to understand the background of what they were seeing. All the action in this play presupposes knowledge of the curse of the House of Atreus. The basis of this is as follows. Thyestes had seduced his brother Atreus' wife; in revenge, Atreus slaughtered his brother's children and served them to him at a banquet. Agamemnon and Menelaus, both kings of Greek states, are sons, elder and younger, of Atreus, and in very elaborate and long-drawn-out ways inherit the curse that descended upon him for his actions. One major problem that occurs is that Menelaus' wife, Helen, flees to Troy with Paris, the incident that triggers the Trojan War. It behooves Agamemnon, as his brother and also the most powerful king in Greece, to attempt to bring Menelaus' wife back. When he sails with a fleet to achieve this, the fleet is becalmed in Aulis and, according to the seer Calchas, the only way he can get the wind he needs is by sacrificing his own daughter, Iphigenia, to the goddess Artemis.

When Agamemnon returns to Greece after the Trojan War, Clytemnestra, his wife, supported by her paramour, Aegisthus, a son of Thyestes, murders her husband; thus Thyestes and Iphigenia are both avenged. This constitutes the main action of the *Agamemnon*.

In *The Libation-Bearers*, second play of the trilogy, Orestes, son of Agamemnon and Clytemnestra, returns to the home of his deceased father (from which he had been banished by Aegisthus in the fear that he would avenge his father). There he is reunited with his sister Electra and, with her encouragement, he finally does avenge their father by murdering their mother Clytemnestra and her lover Aegisthus. The final play, *The Furies*, concerns the torment undergone by Orestes at the hands of the ancient Furies, or avenging deities. At the end, a chord of redemption and reconciliation is struck.

Despite the grim, even gruesome nature of these stories, the author's broad philosophical perspective and sympathy for human suffering together with the grandeur and richly woven tapestry of his poetry created a monument of drama that has survived the ages.

Contents

AGAMEMNON

Dramatis Personae

A WATCHMAN

CHORUS

CLYTEMNESTRA

A HERALD

AGAMEMNON

CASSANDRA

AEGISTHUS

The scene is the Palace of Atreus at Mycenae. In front of the Palace stand statues of the gods, and altars prepared for sacrifices.

A WATCHMAN
>　I pray the gods to quit me of my toils,
>　To close the watch I keep, this livelong year;
>　For as a watch-dog lying, not at rest,
>　Propped on one arm, upon the palace-roof
>　Of Atreus' race, too long, too well I know
>　The starry conclave of the midnight sky,
>　Too well, the splendours of the firmament,
>　The lords of light, whose kingly aspect shows —
>　What time they set or climb the sky in turn —
>　The year's divisions, bringing frost or fire.

>　And now, as ever, am I set to mark
>　When shall stream up the glow of signal-flame,
>　The bale-fire bright, and tell its Trojan tale —
>　*Troy town is ta'en:* such issue holds in hope
>　She in whose woman's breast beats heart of man.

>　Thus upon mine unrestful couch I lie,
>　Bathed with the dews of night, unvisited
>　By dreams — ah me! — for in the place of sleep
>　Stands Fear as my familiar, and repels
>　The soft repose that would mine eyelids seal.
>　And if at whiles, for the lost balm of sleep,
>　I medicine my soul with melody
>　Of trill or song — anon to tears I turn,
>　Wailing the woe that broods upon this home,
>　Not now by honour guided as of old.

>　But now at last fair fall the welcome hour
>　That sets me free, whene'er the thick night glow
>　With beacon-fire of hope deferred no more.
>　All hail!　　　[*A beacon-light is seen reddening the distant sky.*]
>　Fire of the night, that brings my spirit day,
>　Shedding on Argos light, and dance, and song,
>　Greetings to fortune, hail!

Let my loud summons ring within the ears
Of Agamemnon's queen, that she anon
Start from her couch and with a shrill voice cry
A joyous welcome to the beacon-blaze,
For Ilion's fall; such fiery message gleams
From yon high flame; and I, before the rest,
Will foot the lightsome measure of our joy;
For I can say, *My master's dice fell fair —*
Behold! the triple sice, the lucky flame!
Now be my lot to clasp, in loyal love,
The hand of him restored, who rules our home:
Home — but I say no more: upon my tongue
Treads hard the ox o' the adage.
                              Had it voice,
The home itself might soothliest tell its tale;
I, of set will, speak words the wise may learn,
To others, nought remember nor discern.
[*Exit. The* CHORUS *of old men of Mycenae enter, each leaning on a*
        staff. During their song CLYTEMNESTRA *appears in the*
        background, kindling the altars.]

CHORUS
        Ten livelong years have rolled away,
        Since the twin lords of sceptred sway,
        By Zeus endowed with pride of place,
        The doughty chiefs of Atreus' race,
            Went forth of yore,
        To plead with Priam, face to face,
            Before the judgment-seat of War!

        A thousand ships from Argive land
        Put forth to bear the martial band,
        That with a spirit stern and strong
        Went out to right the kingdom's wrong —
        Pealed, as they went, the battle-song,
            Wild as the vultures' cry;
        When o'er the eyrie, soaring high,
        In wild bereavèd agony,
        Around, around, in airy rings,
        They wheel with oarage of their wings,

But not the eyas-brood behold,
That called them to the nest of old;
But let Apollo from the sky,
Or Pan, or Zeus, but hear the cry,
The exile cry, the wail forlorn,
Of birds from whom their home is torn —
On those who wrought the rapine fell,
Heaven sends the vengeful fiends of hell.

Even so doth Zeus, the jealous lord
And guardian of the hearth and board,
Speed Atreus' sons, in vengeful ire,
'Gainst Paris — sends them forth on fire,
Her to buy back, in war and blood,
Whom one did wed but many woo'd!
And many, many, by his will,
The last embrace of foes shall feel,
And many a knee in dust be bowed,
And splintered spears on shields ring loud,
Of Trojan and of Greek, before
That iron bridal-feast be o'er!
But as he willed 'tis ordered all,
And woes, by heaven ordained, must fall —
Unsoothed by tears or spilth of wine
Poured forth too late, the wrath divine
Glares vengeance on the flameless shrine.

And we in gray dishonoured eld,
Feeble of frame, unfit were held
To join the warrior array
That then went forth unto the fray:
And here at home we tarry, fain
Our feeble footsteps to sustain,
Each on his staff — so strength doth wane,
And turns to childishness again.
For while the sap of youth is green,
And, yet unripened, leaps within,
The young are weakly as the old,
And each alike unmeet to hold
The vantage post of war!

And ah! when flower and fruit are o'er,
   And on life's tree the leaves are sere,
   Age wendeth propped its journey drear,
As forceless as a child, as light
And fleeting as a dream of night
Lost in the garish day!

But thou, O child of Tyndareus,
   Queen Clytemnestra, speak! and say
   What messenger of joy to-day
Hath won thine ear? what welcome news,
That thus in sacrificial wise
E'en to the city's boundaries
Thou biddest altar-fires arise?
Each god who doth our city guard,
And keeps o'er Argos watch and ward
   From heaven above, from earth below —
The mighty lords who rule the skies,
The market's lesser deities,
   To each and all the altars glow,
Piled for the sacrifice;
And here and there, anear, afar,
Streams skyward many a beacon-star,
Conjur'd and charm'd and kindled well
By pure oil's soft and guileless spell,
Hid now no more
Within the palace' secret store.

O queen, we pray thee, whatsoe'er,
   Known unto thee, were well revealed,
That thou wilt trust it to our ear,
   And bid our anxious heart be healed!
That waneth now unto despair —
Now, waxing to a presage fair,
Dawns, from the altar, Hope — to scare
From our rent hearts the vulture Care.

List! for the power is mine, to chant on high
   The chiefs' emprise, the strength that omens gave!
List! on my soul breathes yet a harmony,
   From realms of ageless powers, and strong to save!

How brother kings, twin lords of one command,
  Led forth the youth of Hellas in their flower,
Urged on their way, with vengeful spear and brand,
  By warrior-birds, that watched the parting hour.

Go forth to Troy, the eagles seemed to cry —
  And the sea-kings obeyed the sky-kings' word,
When on the right they soared across the sky,
  And one was black, one bore a white tail barred.

High o'er the palace were they seen to soar,
  Then lit in sight of all, and rent and tare,
Far from the fields that she should range no more,
  Big with her unborn brood, a mother-hare.

And one beheld, the soldier-prophet true,
  And the two chiefs, unlike of soul and will,
In the twy-coloured eagles straight he knew,
  And spake the omen forth, for good and ill.

(Ah woe and well-a-day! but be the issue fair!)

Go forth, he cried, *and Priam's town shall fall.*
  Yet long the time shall be; and flock and herd,
The people's wealth, that roam before the wall,
  Shall force hew down, when Fate shall give the word.

But O beware! lest wrath in Heaven abide,
  To dim the glowing battle-forge once more,
And mar the mighty curb of Trojan pride,
  The steel of vengeance, welded as for war!

For virgin Artemis bears jealous hate
  Against the royal house, the eagle-pair,
Who rend the unborn brood, insatiate —
  Yea, loathes their banquet on the quivering hare.

(Ah woe and well-a-day! but be the issue fair!)

For well she loves — the goddess kind and mild —
  The tender new-born cubs of lions bold,
Too weak to range — and well the sucking child
  Of every beast that roams by wood and wold.

So to the Lord of Heaven she prayeth still,
  "Nay, if it must be, be the omen true!
Yet do the visioned eagles presage ill;
  The end be well, but crossed with evil too!"

Healer Apollo! be her wrath controll'd,
  Nor weave the long delay of thwarting gales,
To war against the Danaans and withhold
  From the free ocean-waves their eager sails!

She craves, alas! to see a second life
  Shed forth, a curst unhallowed sacrifice —
'Twixt wedded souls, artificer of strife,
  And hate that knows not fear, and fell device.

At home there tarries like a lurking snake,
  Biding its time, a wrath unreconciled,
A wily watcher, passionate to slake,
  In blood, resentment for a murdered child.

Such was the mighty warning, pealed of yore —
  Amid good tidings, such the word of fear,
What time the fateful eagles hovered o'er
  The kings, and Calchas read the omen clear.

(In strains like his, once more,
Sing woe and well-a-day! but be the issue fair!)

  Zeus — if to The Unknown
    That name of many names seem good —
  Zeus, upon Thee I call.
    Thro' the mind's every road

I passed, but vain are all,
  Save that which names thee Zeus, the Highest One,
    Were it but mine to cast away the load,
The weary load, that weighs my spirit down.

  He that was Lord of old,
In full-blown pride of place and valour bold,
  Hath fallen and is gone, even as an old tale told!
  And he that next held sway,
    By stronger grasp o'erthrown
  Hath pass'd away!
And whoso now shall bid the triumph-chant arise
  To Zeus, and Zeus alone,
He shall be found the truly wise.
'Tis Zeus alone who shows the perfect way
  Of knowledge: He hath ruled,
Men shall learn wisdom, by affliction schooled.

  In visions of the night, like dropping rain,
  Descend the many memories of pain
Before the spirit's sight: through tears and dole
  Comes wisdom o'er the unwilling soul —
  A boon, I wot, of all Divinity,
That holds its sacred throne in strength, above the sky!
    And then the elder chief, at whose command
    The fleet of Greece was manned,
    Cast on the seer no word of hate,
    But veered before the sudden breath of Fate —

  Ah, weary while! for, ere they put forth sail,
  Did every store, each minish'd vessel, fail,
    While all the Achaean host
    At Aulis anchored lay,
  Looking across to Chalics and the coast
  Where refluent waters welter, rock, and sway;
    And rife with ill delay
  From northern Strymon blew the thwarting blast —
    Mother of famine fell,
    That holds men wand'ring still
  Far from the haven where they fain would be! —

And pitiless did waste
Each ship and cable, rotting on the sea,
And, doubling with delay each weary hour,
Withered with hope deferred th' Achæans' warlike flower.

But when, for bitter storm, a deadlier relief,
And heavier with ill to either chief,
Pleading the ire of Artemis, the seer avowed,
    The two Atridæ smote their sceptres on the plain,
    And, striving hard, could not their tears restrain!
    And then the elder monarch spake aloud —
        Ill lot were mine, to disobey!
        And ill, to smite my child, my household's love and pride!
        To stain with virgin blood a father's hands, and slay
        My daughter, by the altar's side!
        'Twixt woe and woe I dwell —
        I dare not like a recreant fly,
And leave the league of ships, and fail each true ally;
        For rightfully they crave, with eager fiery mind,
        The virgin's blood, shed forth to lull the adverse wind —
            God send the deed be well!

Thus on his neck he took
Fate's hard compelling yoke;
Then, in the counter-gale of will abhorr'd, accursed,
    To recklessness his shifting spirit veered —
    Alas! that Frenzy, first of ills and worst,
With evil craft men's souls to sin hath ever stirred!

And so he steeled his heart — ah, well-a-day —
    Aiding a war for one false woman's sake,
        His child to slay,
    And with her spilt blood make
An offering, to speed the ships upon their way!

Lusting for war, the bloody arbiters
Closed heart and ears, and would nor hear nor heed
        The girl-voice plead,
    Pity me, Father! nor her prayers,
        Nor tender, virgin years.

So, when the chant of sacrifice was done,
    Her father bade the youthful priestly train
Raise her, like some poor kid, above the altar-stone,
    From where amid her robes she lay
        Sunk all in swoon away —
Bade them, as with the bit that mutely tames the steed,
    Her fair lips' speech refrain,
Lest she should speak a curse on Atreus' home and seed,

    So, trailing on the earth her robe of saffron dye,
    With one last piteous dart from her beseeching eye
        Those that should smite she smote —
    Fair, silent, as a pictur'd form, but fain
    To plead, *Is all forgot?*
How oft those halls of old,
Wherein my sire high feast did hold,
    Rang to the virginal soft strain,
        When I, a stainless child,
    Sang from pure lips and undefiled,
        Sang of my sire, and all
His honoured life, and how on him should fall
        Heaven's highest gift and gain!
And then — but I beheld not, nor can tell,
    What further fate befel:
But this is sure, that Calchas' boding strain
    Can ne'er be void or vain.
This wage from Justice' hand do sufferers earn,
    The future to discern:
And yet — farewell, O secret of To-morrow!
    Fore-knowledge is fore-sorrow.
Clear with the clear beams of the morrow's sun,
    The future presseth on.
Now, let the house's tale, how dark soe'er,
    Find yet an issue fair! —
So prays the loyal, solitary band
    That guards the Apian land.
                    [*They turn to* CLYTEMNESTRA, *who leaves*
                        the altars and comes forward.]

O queen, I come in reverence of thy sway —
For, while the ruler's kingly seat is void,

The loyal heart before his consort bends.
Now — be it sure and certain news of good,
Or the fair tidings of a flatt'ring hope,
That bids thee spread the light from shrine to shrine,
I, fain to hear, yet grudge not if thou hide.

CLYTEMNESTRA

As saith the adage, *From the womb of Night*
Spring forth, with promise fair, the young child Light.
Ay — fairer even than all hope my news —
By Grecian hands is Priam's city ta'en!

CHORUS

What say'st thou? doubtful heart makes treach'rous ear.

CLYTEMNESTRA

Hear then again, and plainly — Troy is ours!

CHORUS

Thrills thro' my heart such joy as wakens tears.

CLYTEMNESTRA

Ay, thro' those tears thine eye looks loyalty.

CHORUS

But hast thou proof, to make assurance sure?

CLYTEMNESTRA

Go to; I have — unless the god has lied.

CHORUS

Hath some night-vision won thee to belief?

CLYTEMNESTRA

Out on all presage of a slumb'rous soul!

CHORUS
But wert thou cheered by Rumour's wingless word?

CLYTEMNESTRA
Peace — thou dost chide me as a credulous girl.

CHORUS
Say then, how long ago the city fell?

CLYTEMNESTRA
Even in this night that now brings forth the dawn.

CHORUS
Yet who so swift could speed the message here?

CLYTEMNESTRA
From Ida's top Hephaestus, lord of fire,
Sent forth his sign; and on, and ever on,
Beacon to beacon sped the courier-flame.
From Ida to the crag, that Hermes loves,
Of Lemnos; thence unto the steep sublime
Of Athos, throne of Zeus, the broad blaze flared.
Thence, raised aloft to shoot across the sea,
The moving light, rejoicing in its strength,
Sped from the pyre of pine, and urged its way,
In golden glory, like some strange new sun,
Onward, and reached Macistus' watching heights.
There, with no dull delay nor heedless sleep,
The watcher sped the tidings on in turn,
Until the guard upon Messapius' peak
Saw the far flame gleam on Euripus' tide,
And from the high-piled heap of withered furze
Lit the new sign and bade the message on.
Then the strong light, far flown and yet undimmed,
Shot thro' the sky above Asopus' plain,
Bright as the moon, and on Cithaeron's crag
Aroused another watch of flying fire.

And there the sentinels no whit disowned,
But sent redoubled on, the hest of flame —
Swift shot the light, above Gorgopis' bay,
To Aegiplanctus' mount, and bade the peak
Fail not the onward ordinance of fire.
And like a long beard streaming in the wind,
Full-fed with fuel, roared and rose the blaze,
And onward flaring, gleamed above the cape,
Beneath which shimmers the Saronic bay,
And thence leapt light unto Arachne's peak,
The mountain watch that looks upon our town.
Thence to th' Atrides' roof — in lineage fair,
A bright posterity of Ida's fire.
So sped from stage to stage, fulfilled in turn,
Flame after flame, along the course ordained,
And lo! the last to speed upon its way
Sights the end first, and glows unto the goal.
And Troy is ta'en, and by this sign my lord
Tells me the tale, and ye have learned my word.

CHORUS

To heaven, O queen, will I upraise new song:
But, wouldst thou speak once more, I fain would hear
From first to last the marvel of the tale.

CLYTEMNESTRA

Think you — this very morn — the Greeks in Troy,
And loud therein the voice of utter wail!
Within one cup pour vinegar and oil,
And look! unblent, unreconciled, they war.
So in the twofold issue of the strife
Mingle the victor's shout, the captives' moan.
For all the conquered whom the sword has spared
Cling weeping — some unto a brother slain,
Some childlike to a nursing father's form,
And wail the loved and lost, the while their neck
Bows down already 'neath the captive's chain.
And lo! the victors, now the fight is done,
Goaded by restless hunger, far and wide
Range all disordered thro' the town, to snatch

Such victual and such rest as chance may give
Within the captive halls that once were Troy —
Joyful to rid them of the frost and dew,
Wherein they couched upon the plain of old —
Joyful to sleep the gracious night all through,
Unsummoned of the watching sentinel.
Yet let them reverence well the city's gods,
The lords of Troy, tho' fallen, and her shrines;
So shall the spoilers not in turn be spoiled.
Yea, let no craving for forbidden gain
Bid conquerors yield before the darts of greed.
For we need yet, before the race be won,
Homewards, unharmed, to round the course once more.
For should the host wax wanton ere it come,
Then, tho' the sudden blow of fate be spared,
Yet in the sight of gods shall rise once more
The great wrong of the slain, to claim revenge.
Now, hearing from this woman's mouth of mine,
The tale and eke its warning, pray with me,
Luck sway the scale, with no uncertain poise,
For my fair hopes are changed to fairer joys.

CHORUS
A gracious word thy woman's lips have told,
Worthy a wise man's utterance, O my queen;
Now with clear trust in thy convincing tale
I set me to salute the gods with song,
Who bring us bliss to counterpoise our pain.
　　　　　　　　　　　　　　[*Exit* CLYTEMNESTRA.]

Zeus, Lord of heaven! and welcome night
Of victory, that hast our might
　　With all the glories crowned!
On towers of Ilion, free no more,
Hast flung the mighty mesh of war,
　　And closely girt them round,
Till neither warrior may 'scape,
Nor stripling lightly overleap
The trammels as they close, and close,
Till with the grip of doom our foes
　　In slavery's coil are bound!

Zeus, Lord of hospitality,
In grateful awe I bend to thee —
  'Tis thou hast struck the blow!
  At Alexander, long ago,
  We marked thee bend thy vengeful bow,
But long and warily withhold
The eager shaft, which, uncontrolled
And loosed too soon or launched too high,
Had wandered bloodless through the sky.

Zeus, the high God! — whate'er be dim in doubt,
  This can our thought track out —
The blow that fells the sinner is of God,
  And as he wills, the rod
Of vengeance smiteth sore. One said of old,
  The gods list not to hold
A reckoning with him whose feet oppress
  The grace of holiness —
An impious word! for whensoe'er the sire
  Breathed forth rebellious fire —
What time his household overflowed the measure
  Of bliss and health and treasure —
His children's children read the reckoning plain,
  At last, in tears and pain.
On me let weal that brings no woe be sent,
  And therewithal, content!
Who spurns the shrine of Right, nor wealth nor power
  Shall be to him a tower,
To guard him from the gulf: there lies his lot,
  Where all things are forgot.
Lust drives him on — lust, desperate and wild,
  Fate's sin-contriving child —
And cure is none; beyond concealment clear,
  Kindles sin's baleful glare.
As an ill coin beneath the wearing touch
  Betrays by stain and smutch
Its metal false — such is the sinful wight.
  Before, on pinions light,
Fair Pleasure flits, and lures him childlike on,
  While home and kin make moan

Beneath the grinding burden of his crime;
　　Till, in the end of time,
Cast down of heaven, he pours forth fruitless prayer
　　To powers that will not hear.

　　And such did Paris come
　　Unto Atrides' home,
And thence, with sin and shame his welcome to repay,
　　Ravished the wife away —
And she, unto her country and her kin
Leaving the clash of shields and spears and arming ships,
And bearing unto Troy destruction for a dower,
　　And overbold in sin,
Went fleetly thro' the gates, at midnight hour.
　　Oft from the prophets' lips
Moaned out the warning and the wail — Ah woe!
Woe for the home, the home! and for the chieftains, woe!
　　Woe for the bride-bed, warm
Yet from the lovely limbs, the impress of the form
　　Of her who loved her lord, a while ago!
　　　　And woe! for him who stands
Shamed, silent, unreproachful, stretching hands
　　That find her not, and sees, yet will not see,
　　　　That she is far away!
And his sad fancy, yearning o'er the sea,
　　Shall summon and recall
Her wraith, once more to queen it in his hall.
　　And sad with many memories,
The fair cold beauty of each sculptured face —
　　And all to hatefulness is turned their grace,
Seen blankly by forlorn and hungering eyes!
　　And when the night is deep,
Come visions, sweet and sad, and bearing pain
　　Of hopings vain —
Void, void and vain, for scarce the sleeping sight
　　Has seen its old delight,
When thro' the grasps of love that bid it stay
　　It vanishes away
On silent wings that roam adown the ways of sleep.

　　Such are the sights, the sorrows fell,
About our hearth — and worse, whereof I may not tell.

But, all the wide town o'er,
Each home that sent its master far away
     From Hellas' shore,
Feels the keen thrill of heart, the pang of loss, to-day.
     For, truth to say,
The touch of bitter death is manifold!
Familiar was each face, and dear as life,
     That went unto the war,
But thither, whence a warrior went of old,
     Doth nought return —
Only a spear and sword, and ashes in an urn!
     For Ares, lord of strife,
Who doth the swaying scales of battle hold,
War's money-changer, giving dust for gold,
     Sends back, to hearts that held them dear,
Scant ash of warriors, wept with many a tear,
Light to the hand, but heavy to the soul;
     Yea, fills the light urn full
     With what survived the flame —
Death's dusty measure of a hero's frame!

Alas! one cries, and yet alas again!
Our chief is gone, the hero of the spear,
     And hath not left his peer!
Ah woe! another moans — *my spouse is slain,*
     The death of honour, rolled in dust and blood,
Slain for a woman's sin, a false wife's shame!
     Such muttered words of bitter mood
Rise against those who went forth to reclaim;
     Yea, jealous wrath creeps on against th' Atrides' name.

     And others, far beneath the Ilian wall,
Sleep their last sleep — the goodly chiefs and tall,
Couched in the foeman's land, whereon they gave
Their breath, and lords of Troy, each in his Trojan grave.

     Therefore for each and all the city's breast
     Is heavy with a wrath supprest,
As deep and deadly as a curse more loud
     Flung by the common crowd;

And, brooding deeply, doth my soul await
   Tidings of coming fate,
Buried as yet in darkness' womb.
For not forgetful is the high gods' doom
   Against the sons of carnage: all too long
Seems the unjust to prosper and be strong,
   Till the dark Furies come,
And smite with stern reversal all his home,
   Down into dim obstruction — he is gone,
And help and hope, among the lost, is none!

O'er him who vaunteth an exceeding fame,
   Impends a woe condign;
The vengeful bolt upon his eyes doth flame,
   Sped from the hand divine.
This bliss be mine, ungrudged of God, to feel —
   To tread no city to the dust,
   Nor see my own life thrust
Down to a slave's estate beneath another's heel!

Behold, throughout the city wide
Have the swift feet of Rumour hied,
   Roused by the joyful flame:
But is the news they scatter, sooth?
Or haply do they give for truth
   Some cheat which heaven doth frame?
A child were he and all unwise,
   Who let his heart with joy be stirred,
To see the beacon-fires arise,
   And then, beneath some thwarting word,
   Sicken anon with hope deferred.
   The edge of woman's insight still
   Good news from true divideth ill;
Light rumours leap within the bound
That fences female credence round,
But, lightly born, as lightly dies
The tale that springs of her surmise.

Soon shall we know whereof the bale-fires tell,
The beacons, kindled with transmitted flame;

Whether, as well I deem, their tale is true.
Or whether like some dream delusive came
The welcome blaze but to befool our soul.
For lo! I see a herald from the shore
Draw hither, shadowed with the olive-wreath —
And thirsty dust, twin-brother of the clay,
Speaks plain of travel far and truthful news —
No dumb surmise, nor tongue of flame in smoke,
Fitfully kindled from the mountain pyre;
But plainlier shall his voice say, *All is well*,
Or — but away, forebodings adverse, now,
And on fair promise fair fulfilment come!
And whoso for the state prays otherwise,
Himself reap harvest of his ill desire!

Enter HERALD

O land of Argos, fatherland of mine!
To thee at last, beneath the tenth year's sun,
My feet return; the bark of my emprise,
Tho' one by one hope's anchors broke away,
Held by the last, and now rides safely here.
Long, long my soul despaired to win, in death,
Its longed-for rest within our Argive land:
And now all hail, O earth, and hail to thee,
New-risen sun! and hail our country's God,
High-ruling Zeus, and thou, the Pythian lord,
Whose arrows smote us once — smite thou no more!
Was not thy wrath wreaked full upon our heads,
O king Apollo, by Scamander's side?
Turn thou, be turned, be saviour, healer, now!
And hail, all gods who rule the street and mart
And Hermes hail! my patron and my pride,
Herald of heaven, and lord of heralds here!
And Heroes, ye who sped us on our way —
To one and all I cry, *Receive again*
With grace such Argives as the spear has spared.

Ah, home of royalty, belovèd halls,
And solemn shrines, and gods that front the morn!
Benign as erst, with sun-flushed aspect greet

The king returning after many days.
For as from night flash out the beams of day,
So out of darkness dawns a light, a king,
On you, on Argos — Agamemnon comes.
Then hail and greet him well! such meed befits
Him whose right hand hewed down the towers of Troy
With the great axe of Zeus who righteth wrong —
And smote the plain, smote down to nothingness
Each altar, every shrine; and far and wide
Dies from the whole land's face its offspring fair.
Such mighty yoke of fate he set on Troy —
Our lord and monarch, Atreus' elder son,
And comes at last with blissful honour home;
Highest of all who walk on earth to-day —
Not Paris nor the city's self that paid
Sin's price with him, can boast, *Whate'er befal,*
The guerdon we have won outweighs it all.
But at Fate's judgment-seat the robber stands
Condemned of rapine, and his prey is torn
Forth from his hands, and by his deed is reaped
A bloody harvest of his home and land
Gone down to death, and for his guilt and lust
His father's race pays double in the dust.

CHORUS
    Hail, herald of the Greeks, new-come from war.

HERALD
    All hail! not death itself can fright me now.

CHORUS
    Was thine heart wrung with longing for thy land?

HERALD
    So that this joy doth brim mine eyes with tears.

CHORUS
    On you too then this sweet distress did fall ——

HERALD
>How say'st thou? make me master of thy word.

CHORUS
>You longed for us who pined for you again.

HERALD
>Craved the land us who craved it, love for love?

CHORUS
>Yea, till my brooding heart moaned out with pain.

HERALD
>Whence thy despair, that mars the army's joy?

CHORUS
>*Sole cure of wrong is silence*, saith the saw.

HERALD
>Thy kings afar, couldst thou fear other men?

CHORUS
>Death had been sweet, as thou didst say but now.

HERALD
>'Tis true; Fate smiles at last. Throughout our toil,
>These many years, some chances issued fair,
>And some, I wot, were chequered with a curse.
>But who, on earth, hath won the bliss of heaven,
>Thro' time's whole tenor an unbroken weal?
>I could a tale unfold of toiling oars,
>Ill rest, scant landings on a shore rock-strewn,
>All pains, all sorrows, for our daily doom.
>And worse and hatefuller our woes on land;
>For where we couched, close by the foeman's wall,
>The river-plain was ever dank with dews,
>Dropped from the sky, exuded from the earth,

A curse that clung unto our sodden garb,
And hair as horrent as a wild beast's fell.
Why tell the woes of winter, when the birds
Lay stark and stiff, so stern was Ida's snow?
Or summer's scorch, what time the stirless wave
Sank to its sleep beneath the noon-day sun?
Why mourn old woes? their pain has passed away;
And passed away, from those who fell, all care,
For evermore, to rise and live again.
Why sum the count of death, and render thanks
For life by moaning over fate malign?
Farewell, a long farewell to all our woes!
To us, the remnant of the host of Greece,
Comes weal beyond all counterpoise of woe:
Thus boast we rightfully to yonder sun,
Like him far-fleeted over sea and land.
The Argive host prevailed to conquer Troy,
And in the temples of the gods of Greece
Hung up these spoils, a shining sign to Time.
Let those who learn this legend bless aright
The city and its chieftains, and repay
The meed of gratitude to Zeus who willed
And wrought the deed. So stands the tale fulfilled.

CHORUS
Thy words o'erbear my doubt: for news of good,
The ear of age hath ever youth enow:
But those within and Clytemnestra's self
Would fain hear all; glad thou their ears and mine.

Re-enter CLYTEMNESTRA
Last night, when first the fiery courier came,
In sign that Troy is ta'en and razed to earth,
So wild a cry of joy my lips gave out,
That I was chidden — *Hath the beacon watch*
Made sure unto thy soul the sack of Troy?
A very woman thou, whose heart leaps light
At wandering rumours! — and with words like these
They showed me how I strayed, misled of hope.
Yet on each shrine I set the sacrifice,

And, in the strain they held for feminine,
Went heralds thro' the city, to and fro,
With voice of loud proclaim, announcing joy;
And in each fane they lit and quenched with wine
The spicy perfumes fading in the flame.
All is fulfilled: I spare your longer tale —
The king himself anon shall tell me all.
Remains to think what honour best may greet
My lord, the majesty of Argos, home.
What day beams fairer on a woman's eyes
Than this, whereon she flings the portal wide,
To hail her lord, heaven-shielded, home from war?
This to my husband, that he tarry not,
But turn the city's longing into joy!
Yea, let him come, and coming may he find
A wife no other than he left her, true
And faithful as a watch-dog to his home,
His foemen's foe, in all her duties leal,
Trusty to keep for ten long years unmarred
The store whereon he set his master-seal.
Be steel deep-dyed, before ye look to see
Ill joy, ill fame, from other wight, in me!

HERALD
      'Tis fairly said: thus speaks a noble dame,
      Nor speaks amiss, when truth informs the boast.
                                    [*Exit* CLYTEMNESTRA.]

CHORUS
      So has she spoken — be it yours to learn
      By clear interpreters her specious word.
      Turn to me, herald — tell me if anon
      The second well-loved lord of Argos comes?
      Hath Menelaus safely sped with you?

HERALD
      Alas — brief boon unto my friends it were,
      To flatter them, for truth, with falsehoods fair!

CHORUS

Speak joy, if truth be joy, but truth, at worst —
Too plainly, truth and joy are here divorced.

HERALD

The hero and his bark were rapt away
Far from the Grecian fleet? 'tis truth I say.

CHORUS

Whether in all men's sight from Ilion borne,
Or from the fleet by stress of weather torn?

HERALD

Full on the mark thy shaft of speech doth light,
And one short word hath told long woes aright.

CHORUS

But say, what now of him each comrade saith?
What their forebodings, of his life or death?

HERALD

Ask me no more: the truth is known to none,
Save the earth-fostering, all-surveying Sun.

CHORUS

Say, by what doom the fleet of Greece was driven?
How rose, how sank the storm, the wrath of heaven?

HERALD

Nay, ill it were to mar with sorrow's tale
The day of blissful news. The gods demand
Thanksgiving sundered from solicitude.
If one as herald came with rueful face
To say, *The curse has fallen, and the host*
Gone down to death; and one wide wound has reached
The city's heart, and out of many homes
Many are cast and consecrate to death,
Beneath the double scourge, that Ares loves,
The bloody pair, the fire and sword of doom —
If such sore burden weighed upon my tongue,

'Twere fit to speak such words as gladden fiends.
But — coming as he comes who bringeth news
Of safe return from toil, and issues fair,
To men rejoicing in a weal restored —
Dare I to dash good words with ill, and say
How the gods' anger smote the Greeks in storm?
For fire and sea, that erst held bitter feud,
Now swore conspiracy and pledged their faith,
Wasting the Argives worn with toil and war.
Night and great horror of the rising wave
Came o'er us, and the blasts that blow from Thrace
Clashed ship with ship, and some with plunging prow
Thro' scudding drifts of spray and raving storm
Vanished, as strays by some ill shepherd driven.
And when at length the sun rose bright, we saw
Th' Aegæan sea-field flecked with flowers of death,
Corpses of Grecian men and shattered hulls.
For us indeed, some god, as well I deem,
No human power, laid hand upon our helm,
Snatched us or prayed us from the powers of air,
And brought our bark thro' all, unharmed in hull:
And saving Fortune sat and steered us fair,
So that no surge should gulf us deep in brine,
Nor grind our keel upon a rocky shore.

So 'scaped we death that lurks beneath the sea,
But, under day's white light, mistrustful all
Of fortune's smile, we sat and brooded deep,
Shepherds forlorn of thoughts that wandered wild,
O'er this new woe; for smitten was our host,
And lost as ashes scattered from the pyre.
Of whom if any draw his life-breath yet,
Be well assured, he deems of us as dead,
As we of him no other fate forebode.
But heaven save all! If Menelaus live,
He will not tarry, but will surely come:
Therefore if anywhere the high sun's ray
Descries him upon earth, preserved by Zeus,
Who wills not yet to wipe his race away,
Hope still there is that homeward he may wend.
Enough — thou hast the truth unto the end.

CHORUS

> Say, from whose lips the presage fell?
> Who read the future all too well,
>> And named her, in her natal hour,
>> Helen, the bride with war for dower?
> 'Twas one of the Invisible,
>> Guiding his tongue with prescient power.
> On fleet, and host, and citadel,
>> War, sprung from her, and death did lour,
> When from the bride-bed's fine-spun veil
> She to the Zephyr spread her sail.
>
> Strong blew the breeze — the surge closed o'er
> The cloven track of keel and oar,
>> But while she fled, there drove along,
>> Fast in her wake, a mighty throng —
> Athirst for blood, athirst for war,
>> Forward in fell pursuit they sprung,
> Then leapt on Simois' bank ashore,
>> The leafy coppices among —
> No rangers, they, of wood and field,
> But huntsmen of the sword and shield.
>
> Heaven's jealousy, that works its will,
> Sped thus on Troy its destined ill,
>> Well named, at once, the Bride and Bane;
>> And loud rang out the bridal strain;
> But they to whom that song befel
>> Did turn anon to tears again;
> Zeus tarries, but avenges still
>> The husband's wrong, the household's stain!
> He, the hearth's lord, brooks not to see
> Its outraged hospitality.
>
> Even now, and in far other tone,
> Troy chants her dirge of mighty moan,
>> *Woe upon Paris, woe and hate!*
>> *Who wooed his country's doom for mate —*
> This is the burthen of the groan,
>> Wherewith she wails disconsolate

The blood, so many of her own
    Have poured in vain, to fend her fate;
Troy! thou hast fed and freed to roam
A lion-cub within thy home!

A suckling creature, newly ta'en
From mother's teat, still fully fain
    Of nursing care; and oft caressed,
    Within the arms, upon the breast,
Even as an infant, has it lain;
    Or fawns and licks, by hunger pressed,
The hand that will assuage its pain;
    In life's young dawn, a well-loved guest,
A fondling for the children's play,
A joy unto the old and gray.

But waxing time and growth betrays
The blood-thirst of the lion-race,
    And, for the house's fostering care,
    Unbidden all, it revels there,
And bloody recompense repays —
    Rent flesh of kine, its talons tare:
A mighty beast, that slays and slays,
    And mars with blood the household fair,
A God-sent pest invincible,
A minister of fate and hell.

Even so to Ilion's city came by stealth
    A spirit as of windless seas and skies,
A gentle phantom-form of joy and wealth,
    With love's soft arrows speeding from its eyes —
Love's rose, whose thorn doth pierce the soul in subtle wise.

Ah, well-a-day! the bitter bridal-bed,
    When the fair mischief lay by Paris' side!
What curse on palace and on people sped
    With her, the Fury sent on Priam's pride,
By angered Zeus! what tears of many a widowed bride!

Long, long ago to mortals this was told,
    How sweet security and blissful state

Have curses for their children — so men hold —
And for the man of all-too prosperous fate
Springs from a bitter seed some woe insatiate.

Alone, alone, I deem far otherwise;
Not bliss nor wealth it is, but impious deed,
From which that after-growth of ill doth rise!
Woe springs from wrong, the plant is like the seed —
While Right, in honour's house, doth its own likeness breed.

Some past impiety, some gray old crime,
Breeds the young curse, that wantons in our ill,
Early or late, when haps th' appointed time —
And out of light brings power of darkness still,
A master-fiend, a foe, unseen, invincible;

A pride accursed, that broods upon the race
And home in which dark Atè holds her sway —
Sin's child and Woe's, that wears its parents' face;
While Right in smoky cribs shines clear as day,
And decks with weal his life, who walks the righteous way.

From gilded halls, that hands polluted raise,
Right turns away with proud averted eyes,
And of the wealth, men stamp amiss with praise,
Heedless, to poorer, holier temples hies,
And to Fate's goal guides all, in its appointed wise.

Hail to thee, chief of Atreus' race,
Returning proud from Troy subdued!
How shall I greet thy conquering face?
How nor a fulsome praise obtrude,
Nor stint the meed of gratitude?
For mortal men who fall to ill
Take little heed of open truth,
But seek unto its semblance still:
The show of weeping and of ruth

To the forlorn will all men pay,
But, of the grief their eyes display,
Nought to the heart doth pierce its way.
And, with the joyous, they beguile
Their lips unto a feignèd smile,
And force a joy, unfelt the while;
But he who as a shepherd wise
    Doth know his flock, can ne'er misread
Truth in the falsehood of his eyes,
Who veils beneath a kindly guise
    A lukewarm love in deed.
And thou, our leader — when of yore
Thou badest Greece go forth to war
For Helen's sake — I dare avow
That then I held thee not as now;
That to my vision thou didst seem
Dyed in the hues of disesteem.
I held thee for a pilot ill,
And reckless, of thy proper will,
Endowing others doomed to die
With vain and forced audacity!
Now from my heart, ungrudgingly,
To those that wrought, this word be said —
Well fall the labour ye have sped —
Let time and search, O king, declare
What men within thy city's bound
Were loyal to the kingdom's care,
    And who were faithless found.
[*Enter* AGAMEMNON *in a chariot, accompanied by* CASSANDRA.
He speaks without descending.]

AGAMEMNON
        First, as is meet, a king's All-hail be said
        To Argos, and the gods that guard the land —
        Gods who with me availed to speed us home,
        With me availed to wring from Priam's town
        The due of justice. In the court of heaven
        The gods in conclave sat and judged the cause,
        Not from a pleader's tongue, and at the close,
        Unanimous into the urn of doom

This sentence gave, *On Ilion and her men,*
Death: and where hope drew nigh to pardon's urn
No hand there was to cast a vote therein.
And still the smoke of fallen Ilion
Rises in sight of all men, and the flame
Of Atè's hecatomb is living yet,
And where the towers in dusty ashes sink,
Rise the rich fumes of pomp and wealth consumed.
For this must all men pay unto the gods
The meed of mindful hearts and gratitude:
For by our hands the meshes of revenge
Closed on the prey, and for one woman's sake
Troy trodden by the Argive monster lies —
The foal, the shielded band that leapt the wall,
What time with autumn sank the Pleiades.
Yea, o'er the fencing wall a lion sprang
Ravening, and lapped his fill of blood of kings.

Such prelude spoken to the gods in full,
To you I turn, and to the hidden thing
Whereof ye spake but now: and in that thought
I am as you, and what ye say, say I.
For few are they who have such inborn grace,
As to look up with love, and envy not,
When stands another on the height of weal.
Deep in his heart, whom jealousy hath seized,
Her poison lurking doth enhance his load;
For now beneath his proper woes he chafes,
And sighs withal to see another's weal.
I speak not idly, but from knowledge sure —
There be who vaunt an utter loyalty,
That is but as the ghost of friendship dead,
A shadow in a glass, of faith gone by.
One only — he who went reluctant forth
Across the seas with me — Odysseus — he
Was loyal unto me with strength and will,
A trusty trace-horse bound unto my car.
Thus — be he yet beneath the light of day,
Or dead, as well I fear — I speak his praise.

Lastly, whate'er be due to men or gods,
With joint debate, in public council held,
We will decide, and warily contrive
That all which now is well may so abide:
For that which haply needs the healer's art,
That will we medicine, discerning well
If cautery or knife befit the time.

Now, to my palace and the shrines of home,
I will pass in, and greet you first and fair,
Ye gods, who bade me forth, and home again —
And long may Victory tarry in my train!
                    [*Enter* CLYTEMNESTRA, *followed by maidens bearing*
                                              purple robes.]

CLYTEMNESTRA
        Old men of Argos, lieges of our realm,
        Shame shall not bid me shrink lest ye should see
        The love I bear my lord. Such blushing fear
        Dies at the last from hearts of human kind.
        From mine own soul and from no alien lips,
        I know and will reveal the life I bore,
        Reluctant, through the lingering livelong years,
        The while my lord beleaguered Ilion's wall.

        First, that a wife sat sundered from her lord,
        In widowed solitude, was utter woe —
        And woe, to hear how rumour's many tongues
        All boded evil — woe, when he who came
        And he who followed spake of ill on ill,
        Keening *Lost, lost, all lost!* thro' hall and bower.
        Had this my husband met so many wounds,
        As by a thousand channels rumour told,
        No network e'er was full of holes as he.
        Had he been slain, as oft as tidings came
        That he was dead, he well might boast him now
        A second Geryon of triple frame,
        With triple robe of earth above him laid —
        For that below, no matter — triply dead,
        Dead by one death for every form he bore.

And thus distraught by news of wrath and woe,
Oft for self-slaughter had I slung the noose,
But others wrenched it from my neck away.
Hence haps it that Orestes, thine and mine,
The pledge and symbol of our wedded troth,
Stands not beside us now, as he should stand.
Nor marvel thou at this: he dwells with one
Who guards him loyally; 'tis Phocis' king,
Strophius, who warned me erst, *Bethink thee, queen,*
What woes of doubtful issue well may fall!
Thy lord in daily jeopardy at Troy,
While here a populace uncurbed may cry
"Down with the council, down!" bethink thee too,
'Tis the world's way to set a harder heel
On fallen power.
                For thy child's absence then
Such mine excuse, no wily afterthought.
For me, long since the gushing fount of tears
Is wept away; no drop is left to shed.
Dim are the eyes that ever watched till dawn,
Weeping, the bale-fires, piled for thy return,
Night after night unkindled. If I slept,
Each sound — the tiny humming of a gnat,
Roused me again, again, from fitful dreams
Wherein I felt thee smitten, saw thee slain,
Thrice for each moment of mine hour of sleep.
All this I bore, and now, released from woe,
I hail my lord as watch-dog of a fold,
As saving stay-rope of a storm-tossed ship,
As column stout that holds the roof aloft,
As only child unto a sire bereaved,
As land beheld, past hope, by crews forlorn,
As sunshine fair when tempest's wrath is past,
As gushing spring to thirsty wayfarer.
So sweet it is to 'scape the press of pain.
With such salute I bid my husband hail!
Nor heaven be wroth therewith! for long and hard
I bore that ire of old.
                 Sweet lord, step forth,
Step from thy car, I pray — nay, not on earth
Plant the proud foot, O king, that trod down Troy!

Women! why tarry ye, whose task it is
To spread your monarch's path with tapestry?
Swift, swift, with purple strew his passage fair,
That justice lead him to a home, at last,
He scarcely looked to see.
                                    For what remains,
Zeal unsubdued by sleep shall nerve my hand
To work as right and as the gods command.

AGAMEMNON
Daughter of Leda, watcher o'er my home,
Thy greeting well befits mine absence long,
For late and hardly has it reached its end.
Know, that the praise which honour bids us crave,
Must come from others' lips, not from our own:
See too that not in fashion feminine
Thou make a warrior's pathway delicate;
Not unto me, as to some Eastern lord,
Bowing thyself to earth, make homage loud.
Strew not this purple that shall make each step
An arrogance; such pomp beseems the gods,
Not me. A mortal man to set his foot
On these rich dyes? I hold such pride in fear,
And bid thee honour me as man, not god.
Fear not — such footcloths and all gauds apart,
Loud from the trump of Fame my name is blown;
Best gift of heaven it is, in glory's hour,
To think thereon with soberness: and thou —
Bethink thee of the adage, *Call none blest
Till peaceful death have crowned a life of weal.*
'Tis said: I fain would fare unvexed by fear.

CLYTEMNESTRA
Nay, but unsay it — thwart not thou my will!

AGAMEMNON
Know, I have said, and will not mar my word.

CLYTEMNESTRA
Was it fear made this meekness to the gods?

AGAMEMNON
> If cause be cause, 'tis mine for this resolve.

CLYTEMNESTRA
> What, think'st thou, in thy place had Priam done?

AGAMEMNON
> He surely would have walked on broidered robes.

CLYTEMNESTRA
> Then fear not thou the voice of human blame.

AGAMEMNON
> Yet mighty is the murmur of a crowd.

CLYTEMNESTRA
> Shrink not from envy, appanage of bliss.

AGAMEMNON
> War is not woman's part, nor war of words.

CLYTEMNESTRA
> Yet happy victors well may yield therein.

AGAMEMNON
> Dost crave for triumph in this petty strife?

CLYTEMNESTRA
> Yield; of thy grace permit me to prevail!

AGAMEMNON
> Then, if thou wilt, let some one stoop to loose
> Swiftly these sandals, slaves beneath my foot:
> And stepping thus upon the sea's rich dye,

I pray, *Let none among the gods look down*
With jealous eye on me — reluctant all,
To trample thus and mar a thing of price,
Wasting the wealth of garments silver-worth.
Enough hereof: and, for the stranger maid,
Lead her within, but gently: God on high
Looks graciously on him whom triumph's hour
Has made not pitiless. None willingly
Wear the slave's yoke — and she, the prize and flower
Of all we won, comes hither in my train,
Gift of the army to its chief and lord.
— Now, since in this my will bows down to thine,
I will pass in on purples to my home.

CLYTEMNESTRA
A Sea there is — and who shall stay its springs?
And deep within its breast, a mighty store,
Precious as silver, of the purple dye,
Whereby the dipped robe doth its tint renew.
Enough of such, O king, within thy halls
There lies, a store that cannot fail; but I —
I would have gladly vowed unto the gods
Cost of a thousand garments trodden thus,
(Had once the oracle such gift required)
Contriving ransom for thy life preserved.
For while the stock is firm the foliage climbs,
Spreading a shade, what time the dog-star glows;
And thou, returning to thine hearth and home,
Art as a genial warmth in winter hours,
Or as a coolness, when the lord of heaven
Mellows the juice within the bitter grape.
Such boons and more doth bring into a home
The present footstep of its proper lord.
Zeus, Zeus, Fulfilment's lord! my vows fulfil,
And whatsoe'er it be, work forth thy will!
                    [*Exeunt all but* CASSANDRA *and the* CHORUS.]

CHORUS
        Wherefore for ever on the wings of fear
            Hovers a vision drear

Before my boding heart? a strain,
Unbidden and unwelcome, thrills mine ear,
  Oracular of pain.
Not as of old upon my bosom's throne
  Sits Confidence, to spurn
  Such fears, like dreams we know not to discern.
Old, old and gray long since the time has grown,
  Which saw the linkèd cables moor
The fleet, when erst it came to Ilion's sandy shore;
  And now mine eyes and not another's see
    Their safe return.

    Yet none the less in me
The inner spirit sings a boding song,
  Self-prompted, sings the Furies' strain —
    And seeks, and seeks in vain,
    To hope and to be strong!

Ah! to some end of Fate, unseen, unguessed,
  Are these wild throbbings of my heart and breast —
    Yea, of some doom they tell —
      Each pulse, a knell.
    Lief, lief I were, that all
To unfulfilment's hidden realm might fall.

  Too far, too far our mortal spirits strive,
      Grasping at utter weal, unsatisfied —
  Till the fell curse, that dwelleth hard beside,
  Thrust down the sundering wall. Too fair they blow,
    The gales that waft our bark on Fortune's tide!
    Swiftly we sail, the sooner all to drive
    Upon the hidden rock, the reef of woe.

  Then if the hand of caution warily
    Sling forth into the sea
  Part of the freight, lest all should sink below,
  From the deep death it saves the bark: even so,
    Doom-laden though it be, once more may rise
    His household, who is timely wise.

  How oft the famine-stricken field

Is saved by God's large gift, the new year's yield!
But blood of man once spilled,
Once at his feet shed forth, and darkening the plain, —
Nor chant nor charm can call it back again.

So Zeus hath willed:
Else had he spared the leech Asclepius, skilled
To bring man from the dead: the hand divine
Did smite himself with death — a warning and a sign.

Ah me! if Fate, ordained of old,
Held not the will of gods constrained, controlled,
Helpless to us-ward, and apart —
Swifter than speech my heart
Had poured its presage out!
Now, fretting, chafing in the dark of doubt,
'Tis hopeless to unfold
Truth, from fear's tangled skein; and, yearning to proclaim
Its thought, my soul is prophecy and flame.

Re-enter CLYTEMNESTRA
Get thee within thou too, Cassandra, go!
For Zeus to thee in gracious mercy grants
To share the sprinklings of the lustral bowl,
Beside the altar of his guardianship,
Slave among many slaves. What, haughty still?
Step from the car; Alcmena's son, 'tis said,
Was sold perforce and bore the yoke of old.
Ay, hard it is, but, if such fate befall,
'Tis a fair chance to serve within a home
Of ancient wealth and power. An upstart lord,
To whom wealth's harvest came beyond his hope,
Is as a lion to his slaves, in all
Exceeding fierce, immoderate in sway.
Pass in: thou hearest what our ways will be.

CHORUS
Clear unto thee, O maid, is her command,
But thou — within the toils of Fate thou art —
If such thy will, I urge thee to obey;
Yet I misdoubt thou dost nor hear nor heed.

CLYTEMNESTRA
> I wot — unless like swallows she doth use
> Some strange barbarian tongue from oversea —
> My words must speak persuasion to her soul.

CHORUS
> Obey: there is no gentler way than this.
> Step from the car's high seat and follow her.

CLYTEMNESTRA
> Truce to this bootless waiting here without!
> I will not stay: beside the central shrine
> The victims stand, prepared for knife and fire —
> Offerings from hearts beyond all hope made glad.
> Thou — if thou reckest aught of my command,
> 'Twere well done soon: but if thy sense be shut
> From these my words, let thy barbarian hand
> Fulfil by gesture the default of speech.

CHORUS
> No native is she, thus to read thy words
> Unaided: like some wild thing of the wood,
> New-trapped, behold! she shrinks and glares on thee.

CLYTEMNESTRA
> 'Tis madness and the rule of mind distraught,
> Since she beheld her city sink in fire,
> And hither comes, nor brooks the bit, until
> In foam and blood her wrath be champed away.
> See ye to her; unqueenly 'tis for me,
> Unheeded thus to cast away my words.　　[*Exit* CLYTEMNESTRA.]

CHORUS
> But with me pity sits in anger's place.
> Poor maiden, come thou from the car; no way
> There is but this — take up thy servitude.

CASSANDRA

> Woe, woe, alas! Earth, Mother Earth! and thou
> Apollo, Apollo!

CHORUS

> Peace! shriek not to the bright prophetic god,
> Who will not brook the suppliance of woe.

CASSANDRA

> Woe, woe, alas! Earth, Mother Earth! and thou
> Apollo, Apollo!

CHORUS

> Hark, with wild curse she calls anew on him,
> Who stands far off and loathes the voice of wail.

CASSANDRA

> Apollo, Apollo!
> God of all ways, but only Death's to me,
> Once and again, O thou, Destroyer named,
> Thou hast destroyed me, thou, my love of old!

CHORUS

> She grows presageful of her woes to come,
> Slave tho' she be, instinct with prophecy.

CASSANDRA

> Apollo, Apollo!
> God of all ways, but only Death's to me,
> O thou Apollo, thou Destroyer named!
> What way hast led me, to what evil home?

CHORUS

> Know'st thou it not? The home of Atreus' race:
> Take these my words for sooth and ask no more.

CASSANDRA

> Home cursed of God! Bear witness unto me,
>   Ye visioned woes within —

The blood-stained hands of them that smite their kin —
The strangling noose, and, spattered o'er
With human blood, the reeking floor!

CHORUS

How like a sleuth-hound questing on the track,
Keen-scented unto blood and death she hies!

CASSANDRA

Ah! can the ghostly guidance fail,
Whereby my prophet-soul is onwards led?
Look! for their flesh the spectre-children wail,
Their sodden limbs on which their father fed!

CHORUS

Long since we knew of thy prophetic fame, —
But for those deeds we seek no prophet's tongue.

CASSANDRA

God! 'tis another crime —
Worse than the storied woe of olden time,
Cureless, abhorred, that one is plotting here —
A shaming death, for those that should be dear!
Alas! and far away, in foreign land,
He that should help doth stand!

CHORUS

I knew th' old tales, the city rings withal —
But now thy speech is dark, beyond my ken.

CASSANDRA

O wretch, O purpose fell!
Thou for thy wedded lord
The cleansing wave hast poured —
A treacherous welcome!
How the sequel tell?
Too soon 'twill come, too soon, for now, even now,
She smites him, blow on blow!

CHORUS
> Riddles beyond my rede — I peer in vain
> Thro' the dim films that screen the prophecy.

CASSANDRA
> God! a new sight! a net, a snare of hell,
> Set by her hand — herself a snare more fell!
> A wedded wife, she slays her lord,
> Helped by another hand!
> Ye powers, whose hate
> Of Atreus' home no blood can satiate,
> Raise the wild cry above the sacrifice abhorred!

CHORUS
> Why biddest thou some fiend, I know not whom,
> Shriek o'er the house? Thine is no cheering word.
> Back to my heart in frozen fear I feel
> My waning life-blood run —
> The blood that round the wounding steel
> Ebbs slow, as sinks life's parting sun —
> Swift, swift and sure, some woe comes pressing on!

CASSANDRA
> Away, away — keep him away —
> The monarch of the herd, the pasture's pride,
> Far from his mate! In treach'rous wrath,
> Muffling his swarthy horns, with secret scathe
> She gores his fenceless side!
> Hark! in the brimming bath,
> The heavy plash — the dying cry —
> Hark — in the laver — hark, he falls by treachery!

CHORUS
> I read amiss dark sayings such as thine,
> Yet something warns me that they tell of ill.
> O dark prophetic speech,
> Ill tidings dost thou teach
> Ever, to mortals here below!

Ever some tale of awe and woe
Thro' all thy windings manifold
Do we unriddle and unfold!

CASSANDRA

Ah well-a-day! the cup of agony,
Whereof I chant, foams with a draught for me.
Ah lord, ah leader, thou hast led me here —
Was't but to die with thee whose doom is near?

CHORUS

Distraught thou art, divinely stirred,
And wailest for thyself a tuneless lay,
As piteous as the ceaseless tale
Wherewith the brown melodious bird
Doth ever Itys! Itys! wail,
Deep-bowered in sorrow, all its little life-time's day!

CASSANDRA

Ah for thy fate, O shrill-voiced nightingale!
Some solace for thy woes did Heaven afford,
Clothed thee with soft brown plumes, and life apart from wail —
But for my death is edged the double-biting sword!

CHORUS

What pangs are these, what fruitless pain,
    Sent on thee from on high?
Thou chantest terror's frantic strain,
Yet in shrill measured melody.
How thus unerring canst thou sweep along
The prophet's path of boding song?

CASSANDRA

Woe, Paris, woe on thee! thy bridal joy
Was death and fire upon thy race and Troy!
    And woe for thee, Scamander's flood!
    Beside thy banks, O river fair,
    I grew in tender nursing care
    From childhood unto maidenhood!

Now not by thine, but by Cocytus' stream
And Acheron's banks shall ring my boding scream.

CHORUS

   Too plain is all, too plain!
 A child might read aright thy fateful strain.
   Deep in my heart their piercing fang
   Terror and sorrow set, the while I heard
   That piteous, low, tender word,
 Yet to mine ear and heart a crushing pang.

CASSANDRA

   Woe for my city, woe for Ilion's fall!
    Father, how oft with sanguine stain
  Streamed on thine altar-stone the blood of cattle, slain
    That heaven might guard our wall!
    But all was shed in vain.
  Low lie the shattered towers whereas they fell,
  And I — ah burning heart! — shall soon lie low as well.

CHORUS

   Of sorrow is thy song, of sorrow still!
    Alas, what power of ill
  Sits heavy on thy heart and bids thee tell
  In tears of perfect moan thy deadly tale?
 Some woe — I know not what — must close thy piteous wail.

CASSANDRA

   List! for no more the presage of my soul,
   Bride-like, shall peer from its secluding veil;
   But as the morning wind blows clear the east,
   More bright shall blow the wind of prophecy,
   And as against the low bright line of dawn
   Heaves high and higher yet the rolling wave,
   So in the clearing skies of prescience
   Dawns on my soul a further, deadlier woe,
   And I will speak, but in dark speech no more.
   Bear witness, ye, and follow at my side —
   I scent the trail of blood, shed long ago.

Within this house a choir abidingly
Chants in harsh unison the chant of ill;
Yea, and they drink, for more enhardened joy,
Man's blood for wine, and revel in the halls,
Departing never, Furies of the home.
They sit within, they chant the primal curse,
Each spitting hatred on that crime of old,
The brother's couch, the love incestuous
That brought forth hatred to the ravisher.
Say, is my speech or wild and erring now,
Or doth its arrow cleave the mark indeed?
They called me once, *The prophetess of lies,*
The wandering hag, the pest of every door —
Attest ye now, *She knows in very sooth*
The house's curse, the storied infamy.

CHORUS

Yet how should oath — how loyally soe'er
I swear it — aught avail thee? In good sooth,
My wonder meets thy claim: I stand amazed
That thou, a maiden born beyond the seas,
Dost as a native know and tell aright
Tales of a city of an alien tongue.

CASSANDRA

That is my power — a boon Apollo gave.

CHORUS

God though he were, yearning for mortal maid?

CASSANDRA

Ay! what seemed shame of old is shame no more.

CHORUS

Such finer sense suits not with slavery.

CASSANDRA

He strove to win me, panting for my love.

CHORUS
> Came ye by compact unto bridal joys?

CASSANDRA
> Nay — for I plighted troth, then foiled the god.

CHORUS
> Wert thou already dowered with prescience?

CASSANDRA
> Yea — prophetess to Troy of all her doom.

CHORUS
> How left thee then Apollo's wrath unscathed?

CASSANDRA
> I, false to him, seemed prophet false to all.

CHORUS
> Not so — to us at least thy words seem sooth.

CASSANDRA
> Woe for me, woe! Again the agony —
> Dread pain that sees the future all too well
> With ghastly preludes whirls and racks my soul.
> Behold ye — yonder on the palace roof
> The spectre-children sitting — look, such things
> As dreams are made on, phantoms as of babes,
> Horrible shadows, that a kinsman's hand
> Hath marked with murder, and their arms are full —
> A rueful burden — see, they hold them up,
> The entrails upon which their father fed!
>
> For this, for this, I say there plots revenge
> A coward lion, couching in the lair —

Guarding the gate against my master's foot —
My master — mine — I bear the slave's yoke now,
And he, the lord of ships, who trod down Troy,
Knows not the fawning treachery of tongue
Of this thing false and dog-like — how her speech
Glozes and sleeks her purpose, till she win
By ill fate's favour the desirèd chance,
Moving like Atè to a secret end.
O aweless soul! the woman slays her lord —
Woman? what loathsome monster of the earth
Were fit comparison? The double snake —
Or Scylla, where she dwells, the seaman's bane,
Girt round about with rocks? some hag of hell,
Raving a truceless curse upon her kin?
Hark — even now she cries exultingly
The vengeful cry that tells of battle turned —
How fain, forsooth, to greet her chief restored!
Nay then, believe me not: what skills belief
Or disbelief? Fate works its will — and thou
Wilt see and say in ruth, *Her tale was true.*

CHORUS

Ah — 'tis Thyestes' feast on kindred flesh —
I guess her meaning and with horror thrill,
Hearing no shadow'd hint of th' o'er-true tale,
But its full hatefulness: yet, for the rest,
Far from the track I roam, and know no more.

CASSANDRA

'Tis Agamemnon's doom thou shalt behold.

CHORUS

Peace, hapless woman, to thy boding words!

CASSANDRA

Far from my speech stands he who sains and saves.

CHORUS

Ay — were such doom at hand — which God forbid!

CASSANDRA
> Thou praycst idly — these move swift to slay.

CHORUS
> What man prepares a deed of such despite?

CASSANDRA
> Fool! thus to read amiss mine oracles.

CHORUS
> Deviser and device are dark to me.

CASSANDRA
> Dark! all too well I speak the Grecian tongue.

CHORUS
> Ay — but in thine, as in Apollo's strains,
> Familiar is the tongue, but dark the thought.

CASSANDRA
> Ah ah the fire! it waxes, nears me now —
> Woe, woe for me, Apollo of the dawn!
>
> Lo, how the woman-thing, the lioness
> Couched with the wolf — her noble mate afar —
> Will slay me, slave forlorn! Yea, like some witch,
> She drugs the cup of wrath, that slays her lord
> With double death — his recompense for me!
> Ay, 'tis for me, the prey he bore from Troy,
> That she hath sworn his death, and edged the steel!
> Ye wands, ye wreaths that cling around my neck,
> Ye showed me prophetess yet scorned of all —
> I stamp you into death, or e'er I die —
> Down, to destruction!
>   Thus I stand revenged —
> Go, crown some other with a prophet's woe.
> Look! it is he, it is Apollo's self
> Rending from me the prophet-robe he gave.

God! while I wore it yet, thou saw'st me mocked
There at my home by each malicious mouth —
To all and each, an undivided scorn.
The name alike and fate of witch and cheat —
Woe, poverty, and famine — all I bore;
And at this last the god hath brought me here
Into death's toils, and what his love had made,
His hate unmakes me now: and I shall stand
Not now before the altar of my home,
But me a slaughter-house and block of blood
Shall see hewn down, a reeking sacrifice.
Yet shall the gods have heed of me who die,
For by their will shall one requite my doom.
He, to avenge his father's blood outpoured,
Shall smite and slay with matricidal hand.
Ay, he shall come — tho' far away he roam,
A banished wanderer in a stranger's land —
To crown his kindred's edifice of ill,
Called home to vengeance by his father's fall:
Thus have the high gods sworn, and shall fulfil.
And now why mourn I, tarrying on earth,
Since first mine Ilion has found its fate
And I beheld, and those who won the wall
Pass to such issue as the gods ordain?
I too will pass and like them dare to die!
                    [*Turns and looks upon the palace door.*]
Portal of Hades, thus I bid thee hail!
Grant me one boon — a swift and mortal stroke,
That all unwrung by pain, with ebbing blood
Shed forth in quiet death, I close mine eyes.

CHORUS
    Maid of mysterious woes, mysterious lore,
    Long was thy prophecy: but if aright
    Thou readest all thy fate, how, thus unscared,
    Dost thou approach the altar of thy doom,
    As fronts the knife some victim, heaven-controlled?

CASSANDRA
    Friends, there is no avoidance in delay.

CHORUS
> Yet who delays the longest, his the gain.

CASSANDRA
> The day is come — flight were small gain to me!

CHORUS
> O brave endurance of a soul resolved!

CASSANDRA
> That were ill praise, for those of happier doom.

CHORUS
> All fame is happy, even famous death.

CASSANDRA
> Ah sire, ah brethren, famous once were ye!
>> [*She moves to enter the house, then starts back.*]

CHORUS
> What fear is this that scares thee from the house?

CASSANDRA
> Pah!

CHORUS
> What is this cry? some dark despair of soul?

CASSANDRA
> Pah! the house fumes with stench and spilth of blood.

CHORUS
> How? 'tis the smell of household offerings.

CASSANDRA
> 'Tis rank as charnel-scent from open graves.

CHORUS
> Thou canst not mean this scented Syrian nard?

CASSANDRA
> Nay, let me pass within to cry aloud
> The monarch's fate and mine — enough of life.
> Ah friends!
> Bear to me witness, since I fall in death,
> That not as birds that shun the bush and scream
> I moan in idle terror. This attest
> When for my death's revenge another dies,
> A woman for a woman, and a man
> Falls, for a man ill-wedded to his curse.
> Grant me this boon — the last before I die.

CHORUS
> Brave to the last! I mourn thy doom foreseen.

CASSANDRA
> Once more one utterance, but not of wail,
> Though for my death — and then I speak no more.
> Sun! thou whose beam I shall not see again,
> To thee I cry, Let those whom vengeance calls
> To slay their kindred's slayers, quit withal
> The death of me, the slave, the fenceless prey.
>
> Ah state of mortal man! in time of weal,
> A line, a shadow! and if ill fate fall,
> One wet sponge-sweep wipes all our trace away —
> And this I deem less piteous, of the twain.   [*Exit into the palace.*]

CHORUS
> Too true it is! our mortal state
> With bliss is never satiate,
> And none, before the palace high
> And stately of prosperity,
> Cries to us with a voice of fear,
> *Away! 'tis ill to enter here!*
>
> Lo! this our lord hath trodden down,
> By grace of heaven, old Priam's town,

And praised as god he stands once more
    On Argos' shore!
Yet now — if blood shed long ago
Cries out that other blood shall flow —
His life-blood, his, to pay again
The stern requital of the slain —
Peace to that braggart's vaunting vain,
    Who, having heard the chieftain's tale,
    Yet boasts of bliss untouched by bale!

[*A loud cry from within.*]

VOICE OF AGAMEMNON
    O I am sped — a deep, a mortal blow.

CHORUS
    Listen, listen! who is screaming as in mortal agony?

VOICE OF AGAMEMNON
    O! O! again, another, another blow!

CHORUS
    The bloody act is over — I have heard the monarch's cry —
    Let us swiftly take some counsel, lest we too be doomed to die.

ONE OF THE CHORUS
    'Tis best, I judge, aloud for aid to call,
    "Ho! loyal Argives! to the palace, all!"

ANOTHER
    Better, I deem, ourselves to bear the aid,
    And drag the deed to light, while drips the blade.

ANOTHER
    Such will is mine, and what thou say'st I say:
    Swiftly to act! the time brooks no delay.

ANOTHER
    Ay, for 'tis plain, this prelude of their song
    Foretells its close in tyranny and wrong.

ANOTHER

    Behold, we tarry — but thy name, Delay,
    They spurn, and press with sleepless hand to slay.

ANOTHER

    I know not what 'twere well to counsel now —
    Who wills to act, 'tis his to counsel how.

ANOTHER

    Thy doubt is mine: for when a man is slain,
    I have no words to bring his life again.

ANOTHER

    What? e'en for life's sake, bow us to obey
    These house-defilers and their tyrant sway?

ANOTHER

    Unmanly doom! 'twere better far to die —
    Death is a gentler lord than tyranny.

ANOTHER

    Think well — must cry or sign of woe or pain
    Fix our conclusion that the chief is slain?

ANOTHER

    Such talk befits us when the deed we see —
    Conjecture dwells afar from certainty.

LEADER OF THE CHORUS

    I read one will from many a diverse word,
    To know aright, how stands it with our lord!
      [*The scene opens, disclosing* CLYTEMNESTRA, *who comes forward.
        The body of* AGAMEMNON *lies, muffled in a long robe, within a
        silver-sided laver; the corpse of* CASSANDRA *is laid beside him.*]

CLYTEMNESTRA

    Ho, ye who heard me speak so long and oft
    The glozing word that led me to my will —

Hear how I shrink not to unsay it all!
How else should one who willeth to requite
Evil for evil to an enemy
Disguised as friend, weave the mesh straitly round him,
Not to be overleaped, a net of doom?
This is the sum and issue of old strife,
Of me deep-pondered and at length fulfilled.
All is avowed, and as I smote I stand
With foot set firm upon a finished thing!
I turn not to denial: thus I wrought
So that he could nor flee nor ward his doom.
Even as the trammel hems the scaly shoal,
I trapped him with inextricable toils,
The ill abundance of a baffling robe;
Then smote him, once, again — and at each wound
He cried aloud, then as in death relaxed
Each limb and sank to earth; and as he lay,
Once more I smote him, with the last third blow,
Sacred to Hades, saviour of the dead.
And thus he fell, and as he passed away,
Spirit with body chafed; each dying breath
Flung from his breast swift bubbling jets of gore,
And the dark sprinklings of the rain of blood
Fell upon me; and I was fain to feel
That dew — not sweeter is the rain of heaven
To cornland, when the green sheath teems with grain.

Elders of Argos — since the thing stands so,
I bid you to rejoice, if such your will:
Rejoice or not, I vaunt and praise the deed,
And well I ween, if seemly it could be,
'Twere not ill done to pour libations here,
Justly — ay, more than justly — on his corpse
Who filled his home with curses as with wine,
And thus returned to drain the cup he filled.

CHORUS
I marvel at thy tongue's audacity,
To vaunt thus loudly o'er a husband slain.

CLYTEMNESTRA
>Ye hold me as a woman, weak of will,
>And strive to sway me: but my heart is stout,
>Nor fears to speak its uttermost to you,
>Albeit ye know its message. Praise or blame,
>Even as ye list, — I reck not of your words.
>Lo! at my feet lies Agamemnon slain,
>My husband once — and him this hand of mine,
>A right contriver, fashioned for his death.
>Behold the deed!

CHORUS
>Woman, what deadly birth,
>What venomed essence of the earth
>Or dark distilment of the wave,
>   To thee such passion gave,
>Nerving thine hand
>To set upon thy brow this burning crown,
>   The curses of thy land?
>*Our king by thee cut off, hewn down!*
>   *Go forth — they cry — accursèd and forlorn,*
>   *To hate and scorn!*

CLYTEMNESTRA
>O ye just men, who speak my sentence now,
>The city's hate, the ban of all my realm!
>Ye had no voice of old to launch such doom
>On him, my husband, when he held as light
>My daughter's life as that of sheep or goat,
>One victim from the thronging fleecy fold!
>Yea, slew in sacrifice his child and mine,
>The well-loved issue of my travail-pangs,
>To lull and lay the gales that blew from Thrace.
>That deed of his, I say, that stain and shame,
>Had rightly been atoned by banishment;
>But ye, who then were dumb, are stern to judge
>This deed of mine that doth affront your ears.
>Storm out your threats, yet knowing this for sooth,
>That I am ready, if your hand prevail

As mine now doth, to bow beneath your sway:
If God say nay, it shall be yours to learn
By chastisement a late humility.

CHORUS
    Bold is thy craft, and proud
Thy confidence, thy vaunting loud;
Thy soul, that chose a murd'ress' fate,
    Is all with blood elate —
        Maddened to know
The blood not yet avenged, the damnèd spot
    Crimson upon thy brow.
But Fate prepares for thee thy lot —
Smitten as thou didst smite, without a friend,
       To meet thine end!

CLYTEMNESTRA
    Hear then the sanction of the oath I swear —
By the great vengeance for my murdered child,
By Atè, by the Fury unto whom
This man lies sacrificed by hand of mine,
I do not look to tread the hall of Fear,
While in this hearth and home of mine there burns
The light of love — Aegisthus — as of old
Loyal, a stalwart shield of confidence —
As true to me as this slain man was false,
Wronging his wife with paramours at Troy,
Fresh from the kiss of each Chryseis there!
Behold him dead — behold his captive prize,
Seeress and harlot — comfort of his bed,
True prophetess, true paramour — I wot
The sea-bench was not closer to the flesh,
Full oft, of every rower, than was she.
See, ill they did, and ill requites them now.
His death ye know: she as a dying swan
Sang her last dirge, and lies, as erst she lay,
Close to his side, and to my couch has left
A sweet new taste of joys that know no fear.

CHORUS
      Ah woe and well-a-day! I would that Fate —
        Not bearing agony too great,
      Nor stretching me too long on couch of pain —
        Would bid mine eyelids keep
   The morningless and unawakening sleep!
      For life is weary, now my lord is slain,
        The gracious among kings!
Hard fate of old he bore and many grievous things,
      And for a woman's sake, on Ilian land —
Now is his life hewn down, and by a woman's hand.
      O Helen, O infatuate soul,
      Who bad'st the tides of battle roll,
      O'erwhelming thousands, life on life,
      'Neath Ilion's wall!
  And now lies dead the lord of all.
     The blossom of thy storied sin
     Bears blood's inexpiable stain,
     O thou that erst, these halls within,
     Wert unto all a rock of strife,
       A husband's bane!

CLYTEMNESTRA
   Peace! pray not thou for death as though
   Thine heart was whelmed beneath this woe,
   Nor turn thy wrath aside to ban
   The name of Helen, nor recall
   How she, one bane of many a man,
   Sent down to death the Danaan lords,
   To sleep at Troy the sleep of swords,
   And wrought the woe that shattered all.

CHORUS
   Fiend of the race! that swoopest fell
     Upon the double stock of Tantalus,
  Lording it o'er me by a woman's will,
     Stern, manful, and imperious —
      A bitter sway to me!
      Thy very form I see,
    Like some grim raven, perched upon the slain,
  Exulting o'er the crime, aloud, in tuneless strain!

CLYTEMNESTRA
>Right was that word — thou namest well
>The brooding race-fiend, triply fell!
>From him it is that murder's thirst,
>Blood-lapping, inwardly is nursed —
>Ere time the ancient scar can sain,
>New blood comes welling forth again.

CHORUS
>Grim is his wrath and heavy on our home,
>>That fiend of whom thy voice has cried,
>Alas, an omened cry of woe unsatisfied,
>>An all-devouring doom!

>Ah woe, ah Zeus! from Zeus all things befall —
>>Zeus the high cause and finisher of all! —
>Lord of our mortal state, by him are willed
>>All things, by him fulfilled!

>Yet ah my king, my king no more!
>What words to say, what tears to pour
>>Can tell my love for thee?
>The spider-web of treachery
>She wove and wound, thy life around,
>>And lo! I see thee lie,
>And thro' a coward, impious wound
>>Pant forth thy life and die!
>A death of shame — ah woe on woe!
>A treach'rous hand, a cleaving blow!

CLYTEMNESTRA
>My guilt thou harpest, o'er and o'er!
>I bid thee reckon me no more
>>As Agamemnon's spouse.
>The old Avenger, stern of mood
>For Atreus and his feast of blood,
>>Hath struck the lord of Atreus' house,
>And in the semblance of his wife
>>The king hath slain. —

> Yea, for the murdered children's life,
> A chieftain's in requital ta'en.

CHORUS
> Thou guiltless of this murder, thou!
> Who dares such thought avow?
> Yet it may be, wroth for the parent's deed,
> The fiend hath holpen thee to slay the son.
> Dark Ares, god of death, is pressing on
> Thro' streams of blood by kindred shed,
> Exacting the accompt for children dead,
> For clotted blood, for flesh on which their sire did feed.

> Yet ah my king, my king no more!
> What words to say, what tears to pour
>   Can tell my love for thee?
> The spider-web of treachery
> She wove and wound, thy life around,
>   And lo! I see thee lie,
> And thro' a coward, impious wound
>   Pant forth thy life and die!
> A death of shame — ah woe on woe!
> A treach'rous hand, a cleaving blow!

CLYTEMNESTRA
> I deem not that the death he died
>   Had overmuch of shame:
> For this was he who did provide
>   Foul wrong unto his house and name:
> His daughter, blossom of my womb,
> He gave unto a deadly doom,
> Iphigenia, child of tears!
> And as he wrought, even so he fares.
> Nor be his vaunt too loud in hell;
> For by the sword his sin he wrought,
> And by the sword himself is brought
>   Among the dead to dwell.

CHORUS
> Ah whither shall I fly?
> For all in ruin sinks the kingly hall;

Nor swift device nor shift of thought have I,
    To 'scape its fall.
A little while the gentler rain-drops fail;
I stand distraught — a ghastly interval,
Till on the roof-tree rings the bursting hail
Of blood and doom. Even now fate whets the steel
On whetstones new and deadlier than of old,
    The steel that smites, in Justice' hold,
    Another death to deal.
O Earth! that I had lain at rest
And lapped for ever in thy breast,
Ere I had seen my chieftain fall
Within the laver's silver wall,
Low-lying on dishonoured bier!
And who shall give him sepulchre,
And who the wail of sorrow pour?
Woman, 'tis thine no more!
A graceless gift unto his shade
Such tribute, by his murd'ress paid!
Strive not thus wrongly to atone
The impious deed thy hand hath done.
Ah who above the god-like chief
Shall weep the tears of loyal grief?
Who speak above his lowly grave
The last sad praises of the brave?

CLYTEMNESTRA
    Peace! for such task is none of thine.
      By me he fell, by me he died,
    And now his burial rites be mine!
    Yet from these halls no mourners' train
      Shall celebrate his obsequies;
    Only by Acheron's rolling tide
    His child shall spring unto his side,
      And in a daughter's loving wise
    Shall clasp and kiss him once again!

CHORUS
    Lo! sin by sin and sorrow dogg'd by sorrow —
      And who the end can know?

The slayer of to-day shall die to-morrow —
    The wage of wrong is woe.
While Time shall be, while Zeus in heaven is lord,
    His law is fixed and stern;
On him that wrought shall vengeance be outpoured —
    The tides of doom return.
The children of the curse abide within
    These halls of high estate —
And none can wrench from off the home of sin
    The clinging grasp of fate.

CLYTEMNESTRA
    Now walks thy word aright, to tell
    This ancient truth of oracle;
    But I with vows of sooth will pray
    To him, the power that holdeth sway
        O'er all the race of Pleisthenes —
    Tho' dark the deed and deep the guilt,
    With this last blood, my hands have spilt,
        I pray thee let thine anger cease!
    I pray thee pass from us away
        To some new race in other lands,
    There, if thou wilt, to wrong and slay
        The lives of men by kindred hands.

    For me 'tis all sufficient meed,
    Tho' little wealth or power were won,
    So I can say, *'Tis past and done.*
    The bloody lust and murderous,
    The inborn frenzy of our house,
        Is ended, by my deed!   [*Enter* AEGISTHUS.]

AEGISTHUS
    Dawn of the day of rightful vengeance, hail!
    I dare at length aver that gods above
    Have care of men and heed of earthly wrongs.
    I, I who stand and thus exult to see
    This man lie wound in robes the Furies wove,
    Slain in requital of his father's craft.
    Take ye the truth, that Atreus, this man's sire,

The lord and monarch of this land of old,
Held with my sire Thyestes deep dispute,
Brother with brother, for the prize of sway,
And drave him from his home to banishment.
Thereafter, the lorn exile homeward stole
And clung a suppliant to the hearth divine,
And for himself won this immunity —
Not with his own blood to defile the land
That gave him birth. But Atreus, godless sire
Of him who here lies dead, this welcome planned —
With zeal that was not love he feigned to hold
In loyal joy a day of festal cheer,
And bade my father to his board, and set
Before him flesh that was his children once.
First, sitting at the upper board alone,
He hid the fingers and the feet, but gave
The rest — and readily Thyestes took
What to his ignorance no semblance wore
Of human flesh, and ate: behold what curse
That eating brought upon our race and name!
For when he knew what all unhallowed thing
He thus had wrought, with horror's bitter cry
Back-starting, spewing forth the fragments foul,
On Pelops' house a deadly curse he spake —
As darkly as I spurn this damnèd food,
So perish all the race of Pleisthenes!
Thus by that curse fell he whom here ye see,
And I — who else? — this murder wove and planned;
For me, an infant yet in swaddling bands,
Of the three children youngest, Atreus sent
To banishment by my sad father's side:
But Justice brought me home once more, grown now
To manhood's years; and stranger tho' I was,
My right hand reached unto the chieftain's life,
Plotting and planning all that malice bade.
And death itself were honour now to me,
Beholding him in Justice' ambush ta'en.

CHORUS
        Aegisthus, for this insolence of thine
        That vaunts itself in evil, take my scorn.

Of thine own will, thou sayest, thou hast slain
The chieftain, by thine own unaided plot
Devised the piteous death: I rede thee well,
Think not thy head shall 'scape, when right prevails,
The people's ban, the stones of death and doom.

AEGISTHUS

This word from thee, this word from one who rows
Low at the oars beneath, what time we rule,
We of the upper tier? Thou'lt know anon,
'Tis bitter to be taught again in age,
By one so young, submission at the word.
But iron of the chain and hunger's throes
Can minister unto an o'erswoln pride
Marvellous well, ay, even in the old.
Hast eyes, and seest not this? Peace — kick not thus
Against the pricks, unto thy proper pain!

CHORUS

Thou womanish man, waiting till war did cease,
Home-watcher and defiler of the couch,
And arch-deviser of the chieftain's doom!

AEGISTHUS

Bold words again! but they shall end in tears.
The very converse, thine, of Orpheus' tongue:
He roused and led in ecstasy of joy
All things that heard his voice melodious;
But thou as with the futile cry of curs
Wilt draw men wrathfully upon thee. Peace!
Or strong subjection soon shall tame thy tongue.

CHORUS

Ay, thou art one to hold an Argive down —
Thou, skilled to plan the murder of the king,
But not with thine own hand to smite the blow!

AEGISTHUS

That fraudful force was woman's very part,
Not mine, whom deep suspicion from of old

Would have debarred. Now by his treasure's aid
My purpose holds to rule the citizens.
But whoso will not bear my guiding hand,
Him for his corn-fed mettle I will drive
Not as a trace-horse, light-caparisoned,
But to the shafts with heaviest harness bound.
Famine, the grim mate of the dungeon dark,
Shall look on him and shall behold him tame.

CHORUS
Thou losel soul, was then thy strength too slight
To deal in murder, while a woman's hand,
Staining and shaming Argos and its gods,
Availed to slay him? Ho, if anywhere
The light of life smite on Orestes' eyes,
Let him, returning by some guardian fate,
Hew down with force her paramour and her!

AEGISTHUS
How thy word and act shall issue, thou shalt shortly understand.

CHORUS
Up to action, O my comrades! for the fight is hard at hand.
Swift, your right hands to the sword hilt! bare the weapon as for
strife —

AEGISTHUS
Lo! I too am standing ready, hand on hilt for death or life.

CHORUS
'Twas thy word and we accept it: onward to the chance of war!

CLYTEMNESTRA
Nay, enough, enough, my champion! we will smite and slay no
more.
Already have we reaped enough the harvest-field of guilt:

Enough of wrong and murder, let no other blood be spilt.
Peace, old men! and pass away unto the homes by Fate decreed,
Lest ill valour meet our vengeance — 'twas a necessary deed.
But enough of toils and troubles — be the end, if ever, now,
Ere thy talon, O Avenger, deal another deadly blow.
'Tis a woman's word of warning, and let who will list thereto.

AEGISTHUS

But that these should loose and lavish reckless blossoms of the
        tongue,
And in hazard of their fortune cast upon me words of wrong,
And forget the law of subjects, and revile their ruler's word —

CHORUS

Ruler? but 'tis not for Argives, thus to own a dastard lord!

AEGISTHUS

I will follow to chastise thee in my coming days of sway.

CHORUS

Not if Fortune guide Orestes safely on his homeward way.

AEGISTHUS

Ah, well I know how exiles feed on hopes of their return.

CHORUS

Fare and batten on pollution of the right, while 'tis thy turn.

AEGISTHUS

Thou shalt pay, be well assurèd, heavy quittance for thy pride.

CHORUS

Crow and strut, with her to watch thee, like a cock, his mate
        beside!

CLYTEMNESTRA

Heed not thou too highly of them — let the cur-pack growl and
yell:

I and thou will rule the palace and will order all things well.

[*Exeunt.*]

THE LIBATION-BEARERS

Dramatis Personae

ORESTES

CHORUS OF CAPTIVE WOMEN

ELECTRA

A NURSE

CLYTEMNESTRA

AEGISTHUS

AN ATTENDANT

PYLADES

The scene is the Tomb of Agamemnon at Mycenae; afterwards, the Palace of Atreus, hard by the Tomb.

ORESTES

> Lord of the shades and patron of the realm
> That erst my father swayed, list now my prayer,
> Hermes, and save me with thine aiding arm,
> Me who from banishment returning stand
> On this my country; lo, my foot is set
> On this grave-mound, and herald-like, as thou,
> Once and again, I bid my father hear.
> And these twin locks, from mine head shorn, I bring,
> And one to Inachus the river-god,
> My young life's nurturer, I dedicate,
> And one in sign of mourning unfulfilled
> I lay, though late, on this my father's grave.
> For O my father, not beside thy corse
> Stood I to wail thy death, nor was my hand
> Stretched out to bear thee forth to burial.

> What sight is yonder? what this woman-throng
> Hitherward coming, by their sable garb
> Made manifest as mourners? What hath chanced?
> Doth some new sorrow hap within the home?
> Or rightly may I deem that they draw near
> Bearing libations, such as soothe the ire
> Of dead men angered, to my father's grave?
> Nay, such they are indeed; for I descry
> Electra mine own sister pacing hither,
> In moody grief conspicuous. Grant, O Zeus,
> Grant me my father's murder to avenge —
> Be thou my willing champion!
>   Pylades,
> Pass we aside, till rightly I discern
> Wherefore these women throng in suppliance.
>> [*Exeunt* PYLADES *and* ORESTES; *enter the* CHORUS *bearing
>> vessels for libation;* ELECTRA *follows them; they pace slowly
>> towards the tomb of* AGAMEMNON.]

CHORUS

> Forth from the royal halls by high command
>   I bear libations for the dead.

Rings on my smitten breast my smiting hand,
    And all my cheek is rent and red,
Fresh-furrowed by my nails, and all my soul
This many a day doth feed on cries of dole.
    And trailing tatters of my vest,
In looped and windowed raggedness forlorn,
    Hang rent around my breast,
Even as I, by blows of Fate most stern
            Saddened and torn.

    Oracular thro' visions, ghastly clear,
Bearing a blast of wrath from realms below,
And stiffening each rising hair with dread,
        Came out of dream-land Fear,
        And, loud and awful, bade
The shriek ring out at midnight's witching hour,
        And brooded, stern with woe,
Above the inner house, the woman's bower.
And seers inspired did read the dream on oath,
        Chanting aloud *In realms below*
            The dead are wroth;
Against their slayers yet their ire doth glow.

Therefore to bear this gift of graceless worth —
        O Earth, my nursing mother! —
The woman god-accurs'd doth send me forth
        Lest one crime bring another.
Ill is the very word to speak, for none
            Can ransom or atone
For blood once shed and darkening the plain.
        O hearth of woe and bane,
        O state that low doth lie!
Sunless, accursed of men, the shadows brood
    Above the home of murdered majesty.

Rumour of might, unquestioned, unsubdued,
Pervading ears and soul of lesser men,
        Is silent now and dead.
        Yet rules a viler dread;
    For bliss and power, however won,
As gods, and more than gods, dazzle our mortal ken.

Justice doth mark, with scales that swiftly sway,
　　Some that are yet in light;
　　Others in interspace of day and night,
　　　Till Fate arouse them, stay;
And some are lapped in night, where all things are undone.

　　On the life-giving lap of Earth
　　　Blood hath flowed forth;
And now, the seed of vengeance, clots the plain —
　　Unmelting, uneffaced the stain.
And Atè tarries long, but at the last
　　　The sinner's heart is cast
Into pervading, waxing pangs of pain.

　　　Lo, when man's force doth ope
The virgin doors, there is nor cure nor hope
　　For what is lost, — even so, I deem,
Though in one channel ran Earth's every stream,
　　Laving the hand defiled from murder's stain,
　　　　It were vain.

And upon me — ah me! — the gods have laid
　　The woe that wrapped round Troy,
What time they led down from home and kin
　　　Unto a slave's employ —
　　　The doom to bow the head
　　And watch our master's will
　　　Work deeds of good and ill —
To see the headlong sway of force and sin,
　　And hold restrained the spirit's bitter hate,
　　Wailing the monarch's fruitless fate,
Hiding my face within my robe, and fain
Of tears, and chilled with frost of hidden pain.

ELECTRA
　　Hand maidens, orderers of the palace-halls,
　　Since at my side ye come, a suppliant train,
　　Companions of this offering, counsel me

As best befits the time: for I, who pour
Upon the grave these streams funereal,
With what fair word can I invoke my sire?
Shall I aver, *Behold, I bear these gifts*
From well-beloved wife unto her well-beloved lord,
When 'tis from her, my mother, that they come?
I dare not say it: of all words I fail
Wherewith to consecrate unto my sire
These sacrificial honours on his grave.
Or shall I speak this word, as mortals use —
Give back, to those who send these coronals
Full recompense — of ills for acts malign?
Or shall I pour this draught for Earth to drink,
Sans word or reverence, as my sire was slain,
And homeward pass with unreverted eyes,
Casting the bowl away, as one who flings
The household cleansings to the common road?
Be art and part, O friends, in this my doubt,
Even as ye are in that one common hate
Whereby we live attended: fear ye not
The wrath of any man, nor hide your word
Within your breast: the day of death and doom
Awaits alike the freeman and the slave.
Speak, then, if aught thou know'st to aid us more.

CHORUS
Thou biddest; I will speak my soul's thought out,
Revering as a shrine thy father's grave.

ELECTRA
Say then thy say, as thou his tomb reverest.

CHORUS
Speak solemn words to them that love, and pour.

ELECTRA
And of his kin whom dare I name as kind?

CHORUS
> Thyself; and next, whoe'er Aegisthus scorns.

ELECTRA
> Then 'tis myself and thou, my prayer must name.

CHORUS
> Whoe'er they be, 'tis thine to know and name them.

ELECTRA
> Is there no other we may claim as ours?

CHORUS
> Think of Orestes, though far-off he be.

ELECTRA
> Right well in this too hast thou schooled my thought.

CHORUS
> Mindfully, next, on those who shed the blood —

ELECTRA
> Pray on them what? expound, instruct my doubt.

CHORUS
> This; *Upon them some god or mortal come* —

ELECTRA
> As judge or as avenger? speak thy thought.

CHORUS
> Pray in set terms, *Who shall the slayer slay.*

ELECTRA
> Beseemeth it to ask such boon of heaven?

CHORUS
How not, to wreak a wrong upon a foe?

ELECTRA
O mighty Hermes, warder of the shades,
Herald of upper and of under world,
Proclaim and usher down my prayer's appeal
Unto the gods below, that they with eyes
Watchful behold these halls, my sire's of old —
And unto Earth, the mother of all things,
And foster-nurse, and womb that takes their seed.

Lo, I that pour these draughts for men now dead,
Call on my father, who yet holds in ruth
Me and mine own Orestes, *Father, speak —*
How shall thy children rule thine halls again?
Homeless we are and sold; and she who sold
Is she who bore us; and the price she took
Is he who joined with her to work thy death,
Aegisthus, her new lord. Behold me here
Brought down to slave's estate, and far away
Wanders Orestes, banished from the wealth
That once was thine, the profit of thy care,
Whereon these revel in a shameful joy.
Father, my prayer is said; 'tis thine to hear —
Grant that some fair fate bring Orestes home,
And unto me grant these — a purer soul
Than is my mother's, a more stainless hand.

These be my prayers for us; for thee, O sire,
I cry that one may come to smite thy foes,
And that the slayers may in turn be slain.
Cursed is their prayer, and thus I bar its path,
Praying mine own, a counter-curse on them.
And thou, send up to us the righteous boon
For which we pray; thine aids be heaven and earth,
And justice guide the right to victory,   [*To the* CHORUS.]
Thus have I prayed, and thus I shed these streams,
And follow ye the wont, and as with flowers

Crown ye with many a tear and cry the dirge,
Your lips ring out above the dead man's grave.

[*She pours the libations.*]

CHORUS

Woe, woe, woe!
Let the teardrop fall, plashing on the ground
Where our lord lies low:
Fall and cleanse away the cursed libation's stain,
Shed on this grave-mound,
Fenced wherein together, gifts of good or bane
From the dead are found.
Lord of Argos, hearken!
Though around thee darken
Mist of death and hell, arise and hear!
Hearken and awaken to our cry of woe!
Who with might of spear
Shall our home deliver?
Who like Ares bend until it quiver,
Bend the northern bow?
Who with hand upon the hilt himself will thrust with glaive,
Thrust and slay and save?

ELECTRA

Lo! the earth drinks them, to my sire they pass —
Learn ye with me of this thing new and strange.

CHORUS

Speak thou; my breast doth palpitate with fear.

ELECTRA

I see upon the tomb a curl new shorn.

CHORUS

Shorn from what man or what deep-girded maid?

ELECTRA

That may he guess who will; the sign is plain.

CHORUS
> Let me learn this of thee; let youth prompt age.

ELECTRA
> None is there here but I, to clip such gift.

CHORUS
> For they who thus should mourn him hate him sore.

ELECTRA
> And lo! in truth the hair exceeding like —

CHORUS
> Like to what locks and whose? instruct me that.

ELECTRA
> Like unto those my father's children wear.

CHORUS
> Then is this lock Orestes' secret gift?

ELECTRA
> Most like it is unto the curls he wore.

CHORUS
> Yet how dared he to come unto his home?

ELECTRA
> He hath but sent it, clipt to mourn his sire.

CHORUS
> It is a sorrow grievous as his death,
> That he should live yet never dare return.

ELECTRA
> Yea, and my heart o'erflows with gall of grief,
> And I am pierced as with a cleaving dart;

Like to the first drops after drought, my tears
Fall down at will, a bitter bursting tide,
As on this lock I gaze; I cannot deem
That any Argive save Orestes' self
Was ever lord thereof; nor, well I wot,
Hath she, the murd'ress, shorn and laid this lock
To mourn him whom she slew — my mother she,
Bearing no mother's heart, but to her race
A loathing spirit, loathed itself of heaven!
Yet to affirm, as utterly made sure,
That this adornment cometh of the hand
Of mine Orestes, brother of my soul,
I may not venture, yet hope flatters fair!
Ah well-a-day, that this dumb hair had voice
To glad mine ears, as might a messenger,
Bidding me sway no more 'twixt fear and hope,
Clearly commanding, *Cast me hence away,*
Clipped was I from some head thou lovest not;
Or, *I am kin to thee, and here, as thou,*
I come to weep and deck our father's grave.
Aid me, ye gods! for well indeed ye know
How in the gale and counter-gale of doubt,
Like to the seaman's bark, we whirl and stray.
But, if God will our life, how strong shall spring,
From seed how small, the new tree of our home! —
Lo ye, a second sign — these footsteps, look, —
Like to my own, a corresponsive print;
And look, another footmark, — this his own,
And that the foot of one who walked with him.
Mark, how the heel and tendons' print combine,
Measured exact, with mine coincident!
Alas! for doubt and anguish rack my mind.

ORESTES [*approaching suddenly*]
Pray thou, in gratitude for prayers fulfilled,
Fair fall the rest of what I ask of heaven.

ELECTRA
Wherefore? what win I from the gods by prayer?

ORESTES
>This, that thine eyes behold thy heart's desire.

ELECTRA
>On whom of mortals know'st thou that I call?

ORESTES
>I know thy yearning for Orestes deep.

ELECTRA
>Say then, wherein event hath crowned my prayer?

ORESTES
>I, I am he; seek not one more akin.

ELECTRA
>Some fraud, O stranger, weavest thou for me?

ORESTES
>Against myself I weave it, if I weave.

ELECTRA
>Ah, thou hast mind to mock me in my woe!

ORESTES
>'Tis at mine own I mock then, mocking thine.

ELECTRA
>Speak I with thee then as Orestes' self?

ORESTES
>My very face thou see'st and know'st me not,
>And yet but now, when thou didst see the lock
>Shorn for my father's grave, and when thy quest

Was eager on the footprints I had made,
Even I, thy brother, shaped and sized as thou,
Fluttered thy spirit, as at sight of me!
Lay now this ringlet whence 'twas shorn, and judge,
And look upon this robe, thine own hands' work,
The shuttle-prints, the creature wrought thereon —
Refrain thyself, nor prudence lose in joy,
For well I wot, our kin are less than kind.

ELECTRA
O thou that art unto our father's home
Love, grief and hope, for thee the tears ran down,
For thee, the son, the saviour that should be;
Trust thou thine arm and win thy father's halls!
O aspect sweet of fourfold love to me,
Whom upon thee the heart's constraint bids call
As on my father, and the claim of love
From me unto my mother turns to thee,
For she is very hate; to thee too turns
What of my heart went out to her who died
A ruthless death upon the altar-stone;
And for myself I love thee — thee that wast
A brother leal, sole stay of love to me.
Now by thy side be strength and right, and Zeus
Saviour almighty, stand to aid the twain!

ORESTES
Zeus, Zeus! look down on our estate and us,
The orphaned brood of him, our eagle-sire,
Whom to his death a fearful serpent brought
Enwinding him in coils; and we, bereft
And foodless, sink with famine, all too weak
To bear unto the eyrie, as he bore,
Such quarry as he slew. Lo! I and she,
Electra, stand before thee, fatherless,
And each alike cast out and homeless made.

ELECTRA
And if thou leave to death the brood of him
Whose altar blazed for thee, whose reverence

Was thine, all thine, — whence, in the after years,
Shall any hand like his adorn thy shrine
With sacrifice of flesh? the eaglets slain,
Thou wouldst not have a messenger to bear
Thine omens, once so clear, to mortal men;
So, if this kingly stock be withered all,
None on high festivals will fend thy shrine
Stoop thou to raise us! strong the race shall show,
Though puny now it seem, and fallen low.

CHORUS

O children, saviours of your father's home,
Beware ye of your words, lest one should hear
And bear them, for the tongue hath lust to tell,
Unto our masters — whom God grant to me
In pitchy reek of fun'ral flame to see!

ORESTES

Nay, mighty is Apollo's oracle
And shall not fail me, whom it bade to pass
Thro' all this peril; clear the voice rang out
With many warnings, sternly threatening
To my hot heart the wintry chill of pain,
Unless upon the slayers of my sire
I pressed for vengeance: this the god's command —
That I, in ire for home and wealth despoiled,
Should with a craft like theirs the slayers slay:
Else with my very life I should atone
This deed undone, in many a ghastly wise
For he proclaimed unto the ears of men
That offerings, poured to angry power of death,
Exude again, unless their will be done,
As grim disease on those that poured them forth —
As leprous ulcers mounting on the flesh
And with fell fangs corroding what of old
Wore natural form; and on the brow arise
White poisoned hairs, the crown of this disease.
He spake moreover of assailing fiends
Empowered to quit on me my father's blood,
Wreaking their wrath on me, what time in night

Beneath shut lids the spirit's eye sees clear.
The dart that flies in darkness, sped from hell
By spirits of the murdered dead who call
Unto their kin for vengeance, formless fear,
The night-tide's visitant, and madness' curse
Should drive and rack me; and my tortured frame
Should be chased forth from man's community
As with the brazen scorpions of the scourge.
For me and such as me no lustral bowl
Should stand, no spilth of wine be poured to God
For me, and wrath unseen of my dead sire
Should drive me from the shrine; no man should dare
To take me to his hearth, nor dwell with me:
Slow, friendless, cursed of all should be mine end,
And pitiless horror wind me for the grave.
This spake the god — this dare I disobey?
Yea, though I dared, the deed must yet be done;
For to that end diverse desires combine, —
The god's behest, deep grief for him who died,
And last, the grievous blank of wealth despoiled —
All these weigh on me, urge that Argive men,
Minions of valour, who with soul of fire
Did make of fencèd Troy a ruinous heap,
Be not left slaves to two and each a woman!
For he, the man, wears woman's heart; if not,
Soon shall he know, confronted by a man.

[ORESTES, ELECTRA, *and the* CHORUS *gather round the tomb of*
AGAMEMNON *for the invocation which follows.*]

CHORUS

Mighty Fates, on you we call!
Bid the will of Zeus ordain
Power to those, to whom again
Justice turns with hand and aid!
Grievous was the prayer one made —
Grievous let the answer fall!
Where the mighty doom is set,
Justice claims aloud her debt
Who in blood hath dipped the steel,
Deep in blood her meed shall feel!
List an immemorial word —

> Whosoe'er shall take the sword
> Shall perish by the sword.

ORESTES

Father, unblest in death, O father mine!
What breath of word or deed
Can I waft on thee from this far confine
Unto thy lowly bed, —
Waft upon thee, in midst of darkness lying,
Hope's counter-gleam of fire?
Yet the loud dirge of praise brings grace undying
Unto each parted sire.

CHORUS

O child, the spirit of the dead,
Altho' upon his flesh have fed
The grim teeth of the flame,
Is quelled not; after many days
The sting of wrath his soul shall raise,
A vengeance to reclaim!
To the dead rings loud our cry —
Plain the living's treachery —
Swelling, shrilling, urged on high,
The vengeful dirge, for parents slain,
Shall strive and shall attain.

ELECTRA

Hear me too, even me, O father, hear!
Not by one child alone these groans, these tears are shed
Upon thy sepulchre.
Each, each, where thou art lowly laid,
Stands, a suppliant, homeless made:
Ah, and all is full of ill,
Comfort is there none to say!
Strive and wrestle as we may,
Still stands doom invincible.

CHORUS

Nay, if so he will, the god
Still our tears to joy can turn

He can bid a triumph-ode
   Drown the dirge beside this urn;
He to kingly halls can greet
The child restored, the homeward-guided feet.

ORESTES

Ah my father! hadst thou lain
   Under Ilion's wall,
By some Lycian spearman slain,
   Thou hadst left in this thine hall
Honour; thou hadst wrought for us
Fame and life most glorious.
   Over-seas if thou had'st died,
Heavily had stood thy tomb,
   Heaped on high; but, quenched in pride,
Grief were light unto thy home.

CHORUS

Loved and honoured hadst thou lain
   By the dead that nobly fell,
In the under-world again,
   Where are throned the kings of hell,
   Full of sway adorable
Thou hadst stood at their right hand —
Thou that wert, in mortal land,
   By Fate's ordinance and law,
King of kings who bear the crown
   And the staff, to which in awe
Mortal men bow down.

ELECTRA

Nay O father, I were fain
Other fate had fallen on thee.
   Ill it were if thou hadst lain
   One among the common slain,
   Fallen by Scamander's side —
Those who slew thee there should be!
Then, untouched by slavery,
   We had heard as from afar

Deaths of those who should have died
'Mid the chance of war.

CHORUS

O child, forbear! things all too high thou sayest.
Easy, but vain, thy cry!
A boon above all gold is that thou prayest,
An unreached destiny,
As of the blessèd land that far aloof
Beyond the north wind lies;
Yet doth your double prayer ring loud reproof;
A double scourge of sighs
Awakes the dead; th' avengers rise, though late;
Blood stains the guilty pride
Of the accursed who rule on earth, and Fate
Stands on the children's side.

ELECTRA

That hath sped thro' mine ear, like a shaft from a bow!
Zeus, Zeus! it is thou who dost send from below
A doom on the desperate doer — ere long
On a mother a father shall visit his wrong.

CHORUS

Be it mine to upraise thro' the reek of the pyre
The chant of delight, while the funeral fire
Devoureth the corpse of a man that is slain
And a woman laid low!
For who bids me conceal it! out-rending control,
Blows ever stern blast of hate thro' my soul,
And before me a vision of wrath and of bane
Flits and waves to and fro.

ORESTES

Zeus, thou alone to us art parent now.
Smite with a rending blow
Upon their heads, and bid the land be well:
Set right where wrong hath stood; and thou give ear,
O Earth, unto my prayer —
Yea, hear O mother Earth, and monarchy of hell!

CHORUS

Nay, the law is sternly set —
Blood-drops shed upon the ground
Plead for other bloodshed yet;
Loud the call of death doth sound,
Calling guilt of olden time,
A Fury, crowning crime with crime.

ELECTRA

Where, where are ye, avenging powers,
Puissant Furies of the slain?
Behold the relics of the race
Of Atreus, thrust from pride of place!
O Zeus, what home henceforth is ours,
What refuge to attain?

CHORUS

Lo, at your wail my heart throbs, wildly stirred;
Now am I lorn with sadness,
Darkened in all my soul, to hear your sorrow's word.
Anon to hope, the seat of strength, I rise, —
She, thrusting grief away, lifts up mine eyes
To the new dawn of gladness.

ORESTES

Skills it to tell of aught save wrong on wrong,
Wrought by our mother's deed?
Though now she fawn for pardon, sternly strong
Standeth our wrath, and will nor hear nor heed;
Her children's soul is wolfish, born from hers,
And softens not by prayers.

CHORUS

I dealt upon my breast the blow
That Asian mourning women know;
Wails from my breast the fun'ral cry,
The Cissian weeping melody;
Stretched rendingly forth, to tatter and tear,

My clenched hands wander, here and there,
From head to breast; distraught with blows
Throb dizzily my brows.

ELECTRA

Aweless in hate, O mother, sternly brave!
As in a foeman's grave
Thou laid'st in earth a king, but to the bier
No citizen drew near, —
Thy husband, thine, yet for his obsequies,
Thou bad'st no wail arise!

ORESTES

Alas, the shameful burial thou dost speak!
Yet I the vengeance of his shame will wreak —
That do the gods command!
That shall achieve mine hand!
Grant me to thrust her life away, and I
Will dare to die!

CHORUS

List thou the deed! Hewn down and foully torn,
He to the tomb was borne;
Yea, by her hand, the deed who wrought,
With like dishonour to the grave was brought,
And by her hand she strove, with strong desire,
Thy life to crush, O child, by murder of thy sire:
Bethink thee, hearing, of the shame, the pain
Wherewith that sire was slain!

ELECTRA

Yea, such was the doom of my sire; well-a-day,
I was thrust from his side, —
As a dog from the chamber they thrust me away,
And in place of my laughter rose sobbing and tears,
As in darkness I lay.
O father, if this word can pass to thine ears,
To thy soul let it reach and abide!

CHORUS

>Let it pass, let it pierce, through the sense of thine ear,
>>To thy soul, where in silence it waiteth the hour!
>The past is accomplished; but rouse thee to hear
>What the future prepareth; awake and appear,
>>Our champion, in wrath and in power!

ORESTES

>O father, to thy loved ones come in aid.

ELECTRA

>With tears I call on thee.

CHORUS

>>Listen and rise to light!
>Be thou with us, be thou against the foe!
>Swiftly this cry arises — even so
>>Pray we, the loyal band, as we have prayed!

ORESTES

>Let their might meet with mine, and their right with my right.

ELECTRA

>O ye Gods, it is yours to decree.

CHORUS

>Ye call unto the dead; I quake to hear.
>Fate is ordained of old, and shall fulfil your prayer.

ELECTRA

>Alas, the inborn curse that haunts our home,
>>Of Atè's bloodstained scourge the tuneless sound!
>Alas, the deep insufferable doom,
>>The stanchless wound!

ORESTES

>It shall be stanched, the task is ours, —
>>Not by a stranger's, but by kindred hand,

Shall be chased forth the blood-fiend of our land.
 Be this our spoken spell, to call Earth's nether powers!

CHORUS

   Lords of a dark eternity,
   To you has come the children's cry,
   Send up from hell, fulfil your aid
    To them who prayed.

ORESTES

 O father, murdered in unkingly wise,
 Fulfil my prayer, grant me thine halls to sway.

ELECTRA

 To me, too, grant this boon — dark death to deal
 Unto Aegisthus, and to 'scape my doom.

ORESTES

 So shall the rightful feasts that mortals pay
 Be set for thee; else, not for thee shall rise
 The scented reek of altars fed with flesh,
 But thou shalt lie dishonoured: hear thou me!

ELECTRA

 I too, from my full heritage restored,
 Will pour the lustral streams, what time I pass
 Forth as a bride from these paternal halls,
 And honour first, beyond all graves, thy tomb.

ORESTES

 Earth, send my sire to fend me in the fight!

ELECTRA

 Give fair-faced fortune, O Persephone!

ORESTES

 Bethink thee, father, in the laver slain —

ELECTRA
>Bethink thee of the net they handselled for thee!

ORESTES
>Bonds not of brass ensnared thee, father mine.

ELECTRA
>Yea, the ill craft of an enfolding robe.

ORESTES
>By this our bitter speech arise, O sire!

ELECTRA
>Raise thou thine head at love's last, dearest call!

ORESTES
>Yea, speed forth Right to aid thy kinsmen's cause;
>Grip for grip, let them grasp the foe, if thou
>Willest in triumph to forget thy fall.

ELECTRA
>Hear me, O father, once again hear me.
>Lo! at thy tomb, two fledglings of thy brood —
>A man-child and a maid; hold them in ruth,
>Nor wipe them out, the last of Pelops' line.
>For while they live, thou livest from the dead;
>Children are memory's voices, and preserve
>The dead from wholly dying: as a net
>Is ever by the buoyant corks upheld,
>Which save the flex-mesh, in the depth submerged.
>Listen, this wail of ours doth rise for thee,
>And as thou heedest it thyself art saved.

CHORUS
>In sooth, a blameless prayer ye spake at length —
>The tomb's requital for its dirge denied:
>Now, for the rest, as thou art fixed to do,
>Take fortune by the hand and work thy will.

ORESTES
> The doom is set; and yet I fain would ask —
> Not swerving from the course of my resolve, —
> Wherefore she sent these offerings, and why
> She softens all too late her cureless deed?
> An idle boon it was, to send them here
> Unto the dead who recks not of such gifts.
> I cannot guess her thought, but well I ween
> Such gifts are skilless to atone such crime.
> Be blood once spilled, an idle strife he strives
> Who seeks with other wealth or wine outpoured
> To atone the deed. So stands the word, nor fails.
> Yet would I know her thought; speak, if thou knowest.

CHORUS
> I know it, son; for at her side I stood.
> 'Twas the night-wandering terror of a dream
> That flung her shivering from her couch, and bade her —
> Her, the accursed of God — these offerings send.

ORESTES
> Heard ye the dream, to tell it forth aright?

CHORUS
> Yea, from herself; her womb a serpent bare.

ORESTES
> What then the sum and issue of the tale?

CHORUS
> Even as a swaddled child, she lull'd the thing.

ORESTES
> What suckling craved the creature, born full-fanged?

CHORUS
> Yet in her dreams she proffered it the breast.

ORESTES

How? did the hateful thing not bite her teat?

CHORUS

Yea, and sucked forth a blood-gout in the milk.

ORESTES

Not vain this dream — it bodes a man's revenge.

CHORUS

Then out of sleep she started with a cry,
And thro' the palace for their mistress' aid
Full many lamps, that erst lay blind with night,
Flared into light; then, even as mourners use,
She sends these offerings, in hope to win
A cure to cleave and sunder sin from doom.

ORESTES

Earth and my father's grave, to you I call —
Give this her dream fulfilment, and thro' me.
I read it in each part coincident,
With what shall be; for mark, that serpent sprang
From the same womb as I, in swaddling bands
By the same hands was swathed, lipped the same breast,
And sucking forth the same sweet mother's-milk
Infused a clot of blood; and in alarm
She cried upon her wound the cry of pain.
The rede is clear: the thing of dread she nursed,
The death of blood she dies; and I, 'tis I,
In semblance of a serpent, that must slay her.
Thou art my seer, and thus I read the dream.

CHORUS

So do; yet ere thou doest, speak to us,
Biding some act, some, by not acting, aid.

ORESTES

Brief my command: I bid my sister pass
In silence to the house, and all I bid

This my design with wariness conceal,
That they who did by craft a chieftain slay
May by like craft and in like noose be ta'en,
Dying the death which Loxias foretold —
Apollo, king and prophet undisproved.
I with this warrior Pylades will come
In likeness of a stranger, full equipt
As travellers come, and at the palace gates
Will stand, as stranger yet in friendship's bond
Unto this house allied; and each of us
Will speak the tongue that round Parnassus sounds,
Feigning such speech as Phocian voices use.
And what if none of those that tend the gates
Shall welcome us with gladness, since the house
With ills divine is haunted? if this hap,
We at the gate will bide, till, passing by,
Some townsman make conjecture and proclaim,
How? is Aegisthus here, and knowingly
Keeps suppliants aloof, by bolt and bar?
Then shall I win my way; and if I cross
The threshold of the gate, the palace' guard,
And find him throned where once my father sat —
Or if he come anon, and face to face
Confronting, drop his eyes from mine — I swear
He shall not utter, *Who art thou and whence?*
Ere my steel leap, and compassed round with death
Low he shall lie: and thus, full-fed with doom,
The Fury of the house shall drain once more
A deep third draught of rich unmingled blood.
But thou, O sister, look that all within
Be well prepared to give these things event.
And ye — I say 'twere well to bear a tongue
Full of fair silence and of fitting speech
As each beseems the time; and last, do thou,
Hermes the warder-god, keep watch and ward,
And guide to victory my striving sword.   [*Exit with* PYLADES.]

CHORUS
        Many and marvellous the things of fear
                Earth's breast doth bear;
        And the sea's lap with many monsters teems,

And windy levin-bolts and meteor gleams
      Breed many deadly things —
Unknown and flying forms, with fear upon their wings,
      And in their tread is death;
  And rushing whirlwinds, of whose blasting breath
      Man's tongue can tell.
But who can tell aright the fiercer thing,
The aweless soul, within man's breast inhabiting?
Who tell, how, passion-fraught and love-distraught,
The woman's eager, craving thought
Doth wed mankind to woe and ruin fell?
Yea, how the loveless love that doth possess
The woman, even as the lioness,
Doth rend and wrest apart, with eager strife,
      The link of wedded life?

Let him be the witness, whose thought is not borne on light wings
      thro' the air,
But abideth with knowledge, what thing was wrought by Althea's
      despair;
For she marr'd the life-grace of her son, with ill counsel rekindled
      the flame
That was quenched as it glowed on the brand, what time from his
      mother he came,
With the cry of a new-born child; and the brand from the burning
      she won,
For the Fates had foretold it coeval, in life and in death, with
      her son.

Yea, and man's hate tells of another, even Scylla of murderous
      guile,
Who slew for an enemy's sake her father, won o'er by the wile
And the gifts of Cretan Minos, the gauds of the high-wrought gold;
For she clipped from her father's head the lock that should never
      wax old,
As he breathed in the silence of sleep, and knew not her craft and
      her crime —
But Hermes, the guard of the dead, doth grasp her, in fulness of
      time.

And since of the crimes of the cruel I tell, let my singing record
The bitter wedlock and loveless, the curse on these halls
  outpoured,
The crafty device of a woman, whereby did a chieftain fall,
A warrior stern in his wrath, the fear of his enemies all, —
A song of dishonour, untimely! and cold is the hearth that was
  warm,
And ruled by the cowardly spear, the woman's unwomanly arm.

But the summit and crown of all crimes is that which in Lemnos
  befell;
A woe and a mourning it is, a shame and a spitting to tell;
And he that in after time doth speak of his deadliest thought,
Doth say, *It is like to the deed that of old time in Lemnos was
  wrought;*
And loathed of men were the doers, and perished, they and their
  seed,
For the gods brought hate upon them; none loveth the impious
  deed.

It is well of these tales to tell; for the sword in the grasp of Right
With a cleaving, a piercing blow to the innermost heart doth
  smite,
And the deed unlawfully done is not trodden down nor forgot,
When the sinner out-steppeth the law and heedeth the high God
  not;
But Justice hath planted the anvil, and Destiny forgeth the sword
That shall smite in her chosen time; by her is the child restored;
And, darkly devising, the Fiend of the house, world-cursed, will
  repay
The price of the blood of the slain that was shed in the bygone day.
                    [*Enter* ORESTES *and* PYLADES, *in guise of travellers.*]

ORESTES [*knocking at the palace gate*]
    What ho! slave, ho! I smite the palace gate
    In vain, it seems; what ho, attend within, —
    Once more, attend; come forth and ope the halls,
    If yet Aegisthus holds them hospitable.

SLAVE [*from within*]
    Anon, anon!   [Opens the door.]
    Speak, from what land art thou, and sent from whom?

ORESTES
    Go, tell to them who rule the palace-halls,
    Since 'tis to them I come with tidings new —
    (Delay not — Night's dark car is speeding on,
    And time is now for wayfarers to cast
    Anchor in haven, wheresoe'er a house
    Doth welcome strangers) — that there now come forth
    Some one who holds authority within —
    The queen, or, if some man, more seemly were it;
    For when man standeth face to face with man,
    No stammering modesty confounds their speech,
    But each to each doth tell his meaning clear.
                        [*Enter* CLYTEMNESTRA.]

CLYTEMNESTRA
    Speak on, O strangers; have ye need of aught?
    Here is whate'er beseems a house like this —
    Warm bath and bed, tired Nature's soft restorer,
    And courteous eyes to greet you; and if aught
    Of graver import needeth act as well,
    That, as man's charge, I to a man will tell.

ORESTES
    A Daulian man am I, from Phocis bound,
    And as with mine own travel-scrip self-laden
    I went toward Argos, parting hitherward
    With travelling foot, there did encounter me
    One whom I knew not and who knew not me,
    But asked my purposed way nor hid his own,
    And, as we talked together, told his name —
    Strophius of Phocis; then he said, "Good sir,
    Since in all case thou art to Argos bound,
    Forget not this my message, heed it well,
    Tell to his own, *Orestes is no more.*
    And — whatsoe'er his kinsfolk shall resolve,

Whether to bear his dust unto his home,
Or lay him here, in death as erst in life
Exiled for aye, a child of banishment —
Bring me their hest, upon thy backward road;
For now in brazen compass of an urn
His ashes lie, their dues of weeping paid."
So much I heard, and so much tell to thee,
Not knowing if I speak unto his kin
Who rule his home; but well, I deem, it were,
Such news should earliest reach a parent's ear.

CLYTEMNESTRA
Ah woe is me! thy word our ruin tells;
From roof-tree unto base are we despoiled. —
O thou whom nevermore we wrestle down,
Thou Fury of this home, how oft and oft
Thou dost descry what far aloof is laid,
Yea, from afar dost bend th' unerring bow
And rendest from my wretchedness its friends;
As now Orestes — who, a brief while since,
Safe from the mire of death stood warily, —
Was the home's hope to cure th' exulting wrong;
Now thou ordainest, *Let the ill abide*.

ORESTES
To host and hostess thus with fortune blest,
Lief had I come with better news to bear
Unto your greeting and acquaintanceship;
For what goodwill lies deeper than the bond
Of guest and host? and wrong abhorred it were,
As well I deem, if I, who pledged my faith
To one, and greetings from the other had,
Bore not aright the tidings 'twixt the twain.

CLYTEMNESTRA
Whate'er thy news, thou shalt not welcome lack,
Meet and deserved, nor scant our grace shall be.
Hadst thou thyself not come, such tale to tell,
Another, sure, had borne it to our ears.

But lo! the hour is here when travelling guests,
Fresh from the daylong labour of the road,
Should win their rightful due. Take him within   [*To the* Slave.]
To the man-chamber's hospitable rest —
Him and these fellow-farers at his side
Give them such guest-right as beseems our halls;
I bid thee do as thou shalt answer for it.
And I unto the prince who rules our home
Will tell the tale, and, since we lack not friends,
With them will counsel how this hap to bear.
                                              [*Exit* CLYTEMNESTRA.]

CHORUS
              So be it done —
          Sister-servants, when draws nigh
          Time for us aloud to cry
          Orestes and his victory?

              O holy earth and holy tomb
          Over the grave-pit heaped on high,
          Where low doth Agamemnon lie,
              The king of ships, the army's lord!
          Now is the hour — give ear and come,
              For now doth Craft her aid afford,
          And Hermes, guard of shades in hell,
          Stands o'er their strife, to sentinel
              The dooming of the sword.
    I wot the stranger worketh woe within —
    For lo! I see come forth, suffused with tears,
    Orestes' nurse. What ho, Kilissa — thou
    Beyond the doors? Where goest thou? Methinks
    Some grief unbidden walketh at thy side.
                                       [*Enter* KILISSA, *a nurse.*]

KILISSA
          My mistress bids me, with what speed I may,
          Call in Aegisthus to the stranger guests,
          That he may come, and standing face to face,
          A man with men, may thus more clearly learn

This rumour new. Thus speaking, to her slaves
She hid beneath the glance of fictive grief
Laughter for what is wrought — to her desire
Too well; but ill, ill, ill besets the house,
Brought by the tale these guests have told so clear.
And he, God wot, will gladden all his heart
Hearing this rumour. Woe and well-a-day!
The bitter mingled cup of ancient woes,
Hard to be borne, that here in Atreus' house
Befel, was grievous to mine inmost heart,
But never yet did I endure such pain.
All else I bore with set soul patiently;
But now — alack, alack! — Orestes dear,
The day and night-long travail of my soul!
Whom from his mother's womb, a new-born child,
I clasped and cherished! Many a time and oft
Toilsome and profitless my service was,
When his shrill outcry called me from my couch!
For the young child, before the sense is born,
Hath but a dumb thing's life, must needs be nursed
As its own nature bids. The swaddled thing
Hath nought of speech, whate'er discomfort come —
Hunger or thirst or lower weakling need, —
For the babe's stomach works its own relief.
Which knowing well before, yet oft surprised,
'Twas mine to cleanse the swaddling clothes — poor I
Was nurse to tend and fuller to make white;
Two works in one, two handicrafts I took,
When in mine arms the father laid the boy.
And now he's dead — alack and well-a-day!
Yet must I go to him whose wrongful power
Pollutes this house — fair tidings these to him!

CHORUS
  Say then, with what array she bids him come?

KILISSA
  What say'st thou! Speak more clearly for mine ear.

CHORUS
  Bids she bring henchmen, or to come alone?

KILISSA
>She bids him bring a spear-armed body-guard.

CHORUS
>Nay, tell not that unto our loathèd lord,
>But speed to him, put on the mien of joy,
>Say, *Come along, fear nought, the news is good:*
>A bearer can tell straight a twisted tale.

KILISSA
>Does then thy mind in this new tale find joy?

CHORUS
>What if Zeus bid our ill wind veer to fair?

KILISSA
>And how? the home's hope with Orestes dies.

CHORUS
>Not yet — a seer, though feeble, this might see.

KILISSA
>What say'st thou? Know'st thou aught, this tale belying?

CHORUS
>Go, tell the news to him, perform thine hest, —
>What the gods will, themselves can well provide.

KILISSA
>Well, I will go, herein obeying thee;
>And luck fall fair, with favour sent from heaven.   [*Exit.*]

CHORUS
>>Zeus, sire of them who on Olympus dwell,
>>Hear thou, O hear my prayer!

Grant to my rightful lords to prosper well
Even as their zeal is fair!
For right, for right goes up aloud my cry —
Zeus, aid him, stand anigh!

Into his father's hall he goes
To smite his father's foes.
Bid him prevail! by thee on throne of triumph set,
Twice, yea and thrice with joy shall he acquit the debt.

Bethink thee, the young steed, the orphan foal
Of sire beloved by thee, unto the car
Of doom is harnessed fast.
Guide him aright, plant firm a lasting goal,
Speed thou his pace, — O that no chance may mar
The homeward course, the last!

And ye who dwell within the inner chamber
Where shines the storèd joy of gold —
Gods of one heart, O hear ye, and remember;
Up and avenge the blood shed forth of old,
With sudden rightful blow;
Then let the old curse die, nor be renewed
With progeny of blood, —
Once more, and not again, be latter guilt laid low!

O thou who dwell'st in Delphi's mighty cave,
Grant us to see this home once more restored
Unto its rightful lord!
Let it look forth, from veils of death, with joyous eye
Unto the dawning light of liberty;
And Hermes, Maia's child, lend hand to save,
Willing the right, and guide
Our state with Fortune's breeze adown the favouring tide.
Whate'er in darkness hidden lies,
He utters at his will;
He at his will throws darkness on our eye,
By night and eke by day inscrutable.

Then, then shall wealth atone
The ills that here were done.
Then, then will we unbind,
Fling free on wafting wind
Of joy, the woman's voice that waileth now
In piercing accents for a chief laid low;
And this our song shall be —
Hail to the commonwealth restored!
Hail to the freedom won to me!
All hail! for doom hath passed from him, my well-loved lord!

And thou, O child, when Time and Chance agree,
Up to the deed that for thy sire is done!
And if she wail unto thee, *Spare, O son* —
Cry, *Aid, O father* — and achieve the deed,
The horror of man's tongue, the gods' great need!
Hold in thy breast such heart as Perseus had,
The bitter woe work forth,
Appease the summons of the dead,
The wrath of friends on earth;
Yea, set within a sign of blood and doom,
And do to utter death him that pollutes thy home.
[*Enter* AEGISTHUS.]

AEGISTHUS
Hither and not unsummoned have I come;
For a new rumour, borne by stranger men
Arriving hither, hath attained mine ears,
Of hap unwished-for, even Orestes' death.
This were new sorrow, a blood-bolter'd load
Laid on the house that doth already bow
Beneath a former wound that festers deep.
Dare I opine these words have truth and life?
Or are they tales, of woman's terror born,
That fly in the void air, and die disproved?
Canst thou tell aught, and prove it to my soul?

CHORUS
What we have heard, we heard; go thou within
Thyself to ask the strangers of their tale.

Strengthless are tidings, thro' another heard;
Question is his, to whom the tale is brought.

AEGISTHUS

I too will meet and test the messenger,
Whether himself stood witness of the death,
Or tells it merely from dim rumour learnt:
None shall cheat me, whose soul hath watchful eyes.   [*Exit.*]

CHORUS

Zeus, Zeus! what word to me is given?
What cry or prayer, invoking heaven,
      Shall first by me be utterèd?
What speech of craft — nor all revealing,
Nor all too warily concealing —
      Ending my speech, shall aid the deed?
For lo! in readiness is laid
The dark emprise, the rending blade;
      Blood-dropping daggers shall achieve
The dateless doom of Atreus' name,
Or — kindling torch and joyful flame
   In sign of new-won liberty —
      Once more Orestes shall retrieve
      His father's wealth, and, throned on high,
      Shall hold the city's fealty.
      So mighty is the grasp whereby,
Heaven-holpen, he shall trip and throw,
Unseconded, a double foe.
         Ho for the victory!   [*A loud cry within.*]

VOICE OF AEGISTHUS

   Help, help, alas!

CHORUS

   Ho there, ho! how is't within?
   Is't done? is't over? Stand we here aloof
   While it is wrought, that guiltless we may seem
   Of this dark deed; with death is strife fulfilled.   [*Enter a* Slave.]

SLAVE
    O woe, O woe, my lord is done to death!
    Woe, woe, and woe again, Aegisthus gone!
    Hasten, fling wide the doors, unloose the bolts
    Of the queen's chamber. O for some young strength
    To match the need! but aid availeth nought
    To him laid low for ever. Help, help, help!
    Sure to deaf ears I shout, and call in vain
    To slumber ineffectual. What ho!
    The queen! how fareth Clytemnestra's self?
    Her neck too, hers, is close upon the steel,
    And soon shall sink, hewn thro' as justice wills.
                                [*Enter* CLYTEMNESTRA.]

CLYTEMNESTRA
    What ails thee, raising this ado for us?

SLAVE
    I say the dead are come to slay the living.

CLYTEMNESTRA
    Alack, I read thy riddles all too clear —
    We slew by craft and by like craft shall die.
    Swift, bring the axe that slew my lord of old;
    I'll know anon or death or victory —
    So stands the curse, so I confront it here.
              [*Enter* ORESTES, *his sword dropping with blood.*]

ORESTES
    Thee too I seek: for him what's done will serve.

CLYTEMNESTRA
    Woe, woe! Aegisthus, spouse and champion, slain!

ORESTES
    What, lov'st the man? then in his grave lie down,
    Be his in death, desert him nevermore!

CLYTEMNESTRA

    Stay, child, and fear to strike. O son, this breast
    Pillowed thine head full oft, while, drowsed with sleep,
    Thy toothless mouth drew mother's milk from me.

ORESTES

    Can I my mother spare? speak, Pylades.

PYLADES

    Where then would fall the hest Apollo gave
    At Delphi, where the solemn compact sworn?
    Choose thou the hate of all men, not of gods.

ORESTES

    Thou dost prevail; I hold thy counsel good.   [To CLYTEMNESTRA.]
    Follow; I will slay thee at his side.
    With him whom in his life thou lovedst more
    Than Agamemnon, sleep in death, the meed
    For hate where love, and love where hate was due!

CLYTEMNESTRA

    I nursed thee young; must I forego mine eld?

ORESTES

    Thou slew'st my father; shalt thou dwell with me?

CLYTEMNESTRA

    Fate bore a share in these things, O my child!

ORESTES

    Fate also doth provide this doom for thee.

CLYTEMNESTRA

    Beware, O my child, a parent's dying curse.

ORESTES
> A parent who did cast me out to ill!

CLYTEMNESTRA
> Not cast thee out, but to a friendly home.

ORESTES
> Born free, I was by twofold bargain sold.

CLYTEMNESTRA
> Where then the price that I received for thee?

ORESTES
> The price of shame; I taunt thee not more plainly.

CLYTEMNESTRA
> Nay, but recount thy father's lewdness too.

ORESTES
> Home-keeping, chide not him who toils without.

CLYTEMNESTRA
> 'Tis hard for wives to live as widows, child.

ORESTES
> The absent husband toils for them at home.

CLYTEMNESTRA
> Thou growest fain to slay thy mother, child.

ORESTES
> Nay, 'tis thyself wilt slay thyself, not I.

CLYTEMNESTRA
> Beware thy mother's vengeful hounds from hell.

ORESTES
How shall I 'scape my father's, sparing thee?

CLYTEMNESTRA
Living, I cry as to a tomb, unheard.

ORESTES
My father's fate ordains this doom for thee.

CLYTEMNESTRA
Ah, me! this snake it was I bore and nursed.

ORESTES
Ay, right prophetic was thy visioned fear.
Shameful thy deed was — die the death of shame!
                    [*Exit, driving* CLYTEMNESTRA *before him.*]

CHORUS
Lo, even for these I mourn, a double death:
Yet since Orestes, driven on by doom,
Thus crowns the height of murders manifold,
I say, 'tis well — that not in night and death
Should sink the eye and light of this our home.

There came on Priam's race and name
    A vengeance; though it tarried long,
        With heavy doom it came.
Came, too, on Agamemnon's hall
    A lion-pair, twin swordsmen strong.
And last, the heritage doth fall
    To him, to whom from Pythian cave
    The god his deepest counsel gave.
Cry out, rejoice! our kingly hall
        Hath 'scaped from ruin — ne'er again
Its ancient wealth be wasted all
        By two usurpers, sin-defiled —
        An evil path of woe and bane!
On him who dealt the dastard blow
        Comes Craft, Revenge's scheming child.

And hand in hand with him doth go,
   Eager for fight,
The child of Zeus, whom men below
 Call Justice, naming her aright.
   And on her foes her breath
   Is as the blast of death;
For her the god who dwells in deep recess
   Beneath Parnassus' brow,
  Summons with loud acclaim
  To rise, though late and lame,
And come with craft that worketh righteousness.

For even o'er Powers divine this law is strong —
  Thou shalt not serve the wrong.
To that which ruleth heaven beseems it that we bow.
  Lo, freedom's light hath come!
   Lo, now is rent away
The grim and curbing bit that held us dumb.
  Up to the light, ye halls! this many a day
   Too low on earth ye lay.
And Time, the great Accomplisher,
Shall cross the threshold, whensoe'er
He choose with purging hand to cleanse
The palace, driving all pollution thence.
And fair the cast of Fortune's die
Before our state's new lords shall lie,
Not as of old, but bringing fairer doom
  Lo, freedom's light hath come!

[*The scene opens, disclosing* ORESTES *standing over the corpses
of* ÆGISTHUS *and* CLYTEMNESTRA; *in one hand he holds his
sword, in the other the robe in which* AGAMEMNON *was
entangled and slain.*]

ORESTES
 There lies our country's twofold tyranny,
 My father's slayers, spoilers of my home.
 Erst were they royal, sitting on the throne,
 And loving are they yet, — their common fate
 Tells the tale truly, shows their trothplight firm.
 They swore to work mine ill-starred father's death,
 They swore to die together; 'tis fulfilled.
  O ye who stand, this great doom's witnesses,

Behold this too, the dark device which bound
My sire unhappy to his death, — behold
The mesh which trapped his hands, enwound his feet!
Stand round, unfold it — 'tis the trammel-net
That wrapped a chieftain; holds it that he see,
The father — not my sire, but he whose eye
Is judge of all things, the all-seeing Sun!
Let him behold my mother's damnèd deed,
Then let him stand, when need shall be to me,
Witness that justly I have sought and slain
My mother; blameless was Aegisthus' doom —
He died the death law bids adulterers die.
But she who plotted this accursèd thing
To slay her lord, by whom she bare beneath
Her girdle once the burden of her babes,
Beloved erewhile, now turned to hateful foes —
What deem ye of her? or what venomed thing,
Sea-snake or adder, had more power than she
To poison with a touch the flesh unscarred?
So great her daring, such her impious will.
How name her, if I may not speak a curse?
A lion-springe! a laver's swathing cloth,
Wrapping a dead man, twining round his feet —
A net, a trammel, an entangling robe?
Such were the weapon of some strangling thief,
The terror of the road, a cut-purse hound —
With such device full many might he kill,
Full oft exult in heat of villainy.
Ne'er have my house so cursed an indweller —
Heaven send me, rather, childless to be slain!

CHORUS
    Woe for each desperate deed!
    Woe for the queen, with shame of life bereft!
    And ah, for him who still is left,
    Madness, dark blossom of a bloody seed!

ORESTES
    Did she the deed or not? this robe gives proof,
    Imbrued with blood that bathed Aegisthus' sword:

Look, how the spurted stain combines with time
To blur the many dyes that once adorned
Its pattern manifold! I now stand here,
Made glad, made sad with blood, exulting, wailing —
Hear, O thou woven web that slew my sire!
I grieve for deed and death and all my home —
Victor, pollution's damnèd stain for prize.

CHORUS

Alas, that none of mortal men
Can pass his life untouched by pain!
Behold, one woe is here —
Another loometh near.

ORESTES

Hark ye and learn — for what the end shall be
For me I know not: breaking from the curb
My spirit whirls me off, a conquered prey,
Borne as a charioteer by steeds distraught
Far from the course, and madness in my breast
Burneth to chant its song, and leap, and rave —
Hark ye and learn, friends, ere my reason goes!
I say that rightfully I slew my mother,
A thing God-scorned, that foully slew my sire
And chiefest wizard of the spell that bound me
Unto this deed I name the Pythian seer
Apollo, who foretold that if I slew,
The guilt of murder done should pass from me;
But if I spared, the fate that should be mine
I dare not blazon forth — the bow of speech
Can reach not to the mark, that doom to tell.
And now behold me, how with branch and crown
I pass, a suppliant made meet to go
Unto Earth's midmost shrine, the holy ground
Of Loxias, and that renownèd light
Of ever-burning fire, to 'scape the doom
Of kindred murder: to no other shrine
(So Loxias bade) may I for refuge turn.
Bear witness, Argives, in the after time,
How came on me this dread fatality.

Living, I pass a banished wanderer hence,
To leave in death the memory of this cry.

CHORUS

Nay, but the deed is well; link not thy lips
To speech ill-starred, nor vent ill-boding words —
Who hast to Argos her full freedom given,
Lopping two serpents' heads with timely blow.

ORESTES

Look, look, alas!
Handmaidens, see — what Gorgon shapes throng up;
Dusky their robes and all their hair enwound —
Snakes coiled with snakes — off, off, I must away!

CHORUS

Most loyal of all sons unto thy sire,
What visions thus distract thee? Hold, abide;
Great was thy victory, and shalt thou fear?

ORESTES

These are no dreams, void shapes of haunting ill,
But clear to sight my mother's hell-hounds come!

CHORUS

Nay, the fresh bloodshed still imbrues thine hands,
And thence distraction sinks into thy soul.

ORESTES

O king Apollo — see, they swarm and throng —
Black blood of hatred dripping from their eyes!

CHORUS

One remedy thou hast; go, touch the shrine
Of Loxias, and rid thee of these woes.

ORESTES

Ye can behold them not, but I behold them.
Up and away! I dare abide no more.   [*Exit.*]

CHORUS
>   Farewell then as thou mayst, — the god thy friend
>   Guard thee and aid with chances favouring.
>
>   Behold, the storm of woe divine
>   That the raves and beats on Atreus' line
>   Its great third blast hath blown.
>   First was Thyestes' loathly woe —
>   The rueful feast of long ago,
>   On children's flesh, unknown.
>   And next the kingly chief's despite,
>   When he who led the Greeks to fight
>   Was in the bath hewn down.
>   And now the offspring of the race
>   Stands in the third, the saviour's place,
>   To save — or to consume?
>   O whither, ere it be fulfilled,
>   Ere its fierce blast be hushed and stilled,
>   Shall blow the wind of doom?   [*Exeunt.*]

THE FURIES

Dramatis Personae

THE PYTHIAN PRIESTESS

APOLLO

ORESTES

THE GHOST OF CLYTEMNESTRA

CHORUS OF FURIES

ATHENA

ATTENDANTS OF ATHENA

TWELVE ATHENIAN CITIZENS

*The scene of the drama is the Temple of Apollo, at Delphi:
afterwards, the Temple of Athena, on the Acropolis of
Athens, and the adjoining Areopagus.*

The Temple at Delphi

THE PYTHIAN PRIESTESS
    First, in this prayer, of all the gods I name
    The prophet-mother Earth; and Themis next,
    Second who sat — for so with truth is said —
    On this her mother's shrine oracular.
    Then by her grace, who unconstrained allowed,
    There sat thereon another child of Earth —
    Titanian Phoebe. She, in after time,
    Gave o'er the throne, as birthgift to a god,
    Phoebus, who in his own bears Phoebe's name.
    He from the lake and ridge of Delos' isle
    Steered to the port of Pallas' Attic shores,
    The home of ships; and thence he passed and came
    Unto this land and to Parnassus' shrine.
    And at his side, with awe revering him,
    There went the children of Hephaestus' seed,
    The hewers of the sacred way, who tame
    The stubborn tract that erst was wilderness.
      And all this folk, and Delphos, chieftain-king
    Of this their land, with honour gave him home;
    And in his breast Zeus set a prophet's soul,
    And gave to him this throne, whereon he sits,
    Fourth prophet of the shrine, and, Loxias hight,
    Gives voice to that which Zeus his sire decrees.

    Such gods I name in my preluding prayer,
    And after them, I call with honour due
    On Pallas, wardress of the fane, and Nymphs
    Who dwell around the rock Corycian,
    Where in the hollow cave, the wild birds' haunt,
    Wander the feet of lesser gods; and there,
    Right well I know it, Bromian Bacchus dwells,
    Since he in godship led his Maenad host,
    Devising death for Pentheus, whom they rent
    Piecemeal, as hare among the hounds. And last,

I call on Pleistus' springs, Poseidon's might,
And Zeus most high, the great Accomplisher.
Then as a seeress to the sacred chair
I pass and sit; and may the powers divine
Make this mine entrance fruitful in response
Beyond each former advent, triply blest.
And if there stand without, from Hellas bound,
Men seeking oracles, let each pass in
In order of the lot, as use allows;
For the god guides whate'er my tongue proclaims.

> [*She goes into the interior of the temple; after a
> short interval, she returns in great fear.*]

Things fell to speak of, fell for eyes to see,
Have sped me forth again from Loxias' shrine,
With strength unstrung, moving erect no more,
But aiding with my hands my failing feet,
Unnerved by fear. A beldame's force is naught —
Is as a child's, when age and fear combine.
For as I pace towards the inmost fane
Bay-filleted by many a suppliant's hand,
Lo, at the central altar I descry
One crouching as for refuge — yea, a man
Abhorred of heaven; and from his hands, wherein
A sword new-drawn he holds, blood reeked and fell:
A wand he bears, the olive's topmost bough,
Twined as of purpose with a deep close tuft
Of whitest wool. This, that I plainly saw,
Plainly I tell. But lo, in front of him,
Crouched on the altar-steps, a grisly band
Of women slumbers — not like women they,
But Gorgons rather; nay, that word is weak,
Nor may I match the Gorgons' shape with theirs!
Such have I seen in painted semblance erst —
Winged Harpies, snatching food from Phineus' board, —
But these are wingless, black, and all their shape
The eye's abomination to behold.
Fell is the breath — let none draw nigh to it —
Wherewith they snort in slumber; from their eyes
Exude the damnèd drops of poisonous ire:
And such their garb as none should dare to bring
To statues of the gods or homes of men.

I wot not of the tribe wherefrom can come
So fell a legion, nor in what land Earth
Could rear, unharmed, such creatures, nor avow
That she had travailed and brought forth death.
But, for the rest, be all these things a care
Unto the mighty Loxias, the lord
Of this our shrine: healer and prophet he,
Discerner he of portents, and the cleanser
Of other homes — behold, his own to cleanse!   [*Exit.*]

> [*The scene opens, disclosing the interior of the temple:* ORESTES
> *clings to the central altar; the* FURIES *lie slumbering at a
> little distance;* APOLLO *and* HERMES *appear from the
> innermost shrine.*]

APOLLO

Lo, I desert thee never: to the end,
Hard at thy side as now, or sundered far,
I am thy guard, and to thine enemies
Implacably oppose me: look on them,
These greedy fiends, beneath my craft subdued!
See, they are fallen on sleep, these beldames old,
Unto whose grim and wizened maidenhood
Nor god nor man nor beast can e'er draw near.
Yea, evil were they born, for evil's doom,
Evil the dark abyss of Tartarus
Wherein they dwell, and they themselves the hate
Of men on earth, and of Olympian gods.
But thou, flee far and with unfaltering speed;
For they shall hunt thee through the mainland wide
Where'er throughout the tract of travelled earth
Thy foot may roam, and o'er and o'er the seas
And island homes of men. Faint not nor fail,
Too soon and timidly within thy breast
Shepherding thoughts forlorn of this thy toil;
But unto Pallas' city go, and there
Crouch at her shrine, and in thine arms enfold
Her ancient image: there we well shall find
Meet judges for this cause and suasive pleas,
Skilled to contrive for thee deliverance
From all this woe. Be such my pledge to thee,
For by my hest thou didst thy mother slay.

ORESTES

> O king Apollo, since right well thou know'st
> What justice bids, have heed, fulfil the same, —
> Thy strength is all-sufficient to achieve.

APOLLO

> Have thou too heed, nor let thy fear prevail
> Above thy will. And do thou guard him, Hermes,
> Whose blood is brother unto mine, whose sire
> The same high God. Men call thee guide and guard,
> Guide therefore thou and guard my suppliant;
> For Zeus himself reveres the outlaw's right,
> Boon of fair escort, upon man conferred.

> > [*Exeunt* APOLLO, HERMES, *and* ORESTES.
> > *the* GHOST OF CLYTEMNESTRA *rises.*]

GHOST OF CLYTEMNESTRA

> Sleep on! awake! what skills your sleep to me —
> Me, among all the dead by you dishonoured —
> Me from whom never, in the world of death,
> Dieth this curse, *'Tis she who smote and slew,*
> And shamed and scorned I roam? Awake, and hear
> My plaint of dead men's hate intolerable.
> Me, sternly slain by them that should have loved,
> Me doth no god arouse him to avenge,
> Hewn down in blood by matricidal hands.
> Mark ye these wounds from which the heart's blood ran,
> And by whose hand, bethink ye! for the sense
> When shut in sleep hath then the spirit-sight,
> But in the day the inward eye is blind.
> List, ye who drank so oft with lapping tongue
> The wineless draught by me outpoured to soothe
> Your vengeful ire! how oft on kindled shrine
> I laid the feast of darkness, at the hour
> Abhorred of every god but you alone!
> Lo, all my service trampled down and scorned!
> And he hath baulked your chase, as stag the hounds;
> Yea, lightly bounding from the circling toils,
> Hath wried his face in scorn, and flieth far.
> Awake and hear — for mine own soul I cry —

Awake, ye powers of hell! the wandering ghost
That once was Clytemnestra calls — Arise!
                    [*The* FURIES *mutter grimly, as in a dream.*]
Mutter and murmur! He hath flown afar —
My kin have gods to guard them, I have none!
                        [*The* FURIES *mutter as before.*]
O drowsed in sleep too deep to heed my pain!
Orestes flies, who me, his mother, slew.
                    [*The* FURIES *give a confused cry.*]
Yelping, and drowsed again? Up and be doing
That which alone is yours, the deed of hell!
                    [*The* FURIES *give another cry.*]
Lo, sleep and toil, the sworn confederates,
Have quelled your dragon-anger, once so fell!

THE FURIES [*muttering more fiercely and loudly*]
Seize, seize, seize, seize — mark, yonder!

GHOST
In dreams ye chase a prey, and like some hound,
That even in sleep doth ply his woodland toil,
Ye bell and bay. What do ye, sleeping here?
Be not o'ercome with toil, nor sleep-subdued,
Be heedless of my wrong. Up! thrill your heart
With the just chidings of my tongue, — such words
Are as a spur to purpose firmly held.
Blow forth on him the breath of wrath and blood,
Scorch him with reek of fire that burns in you,
Waste him with new pursuit — swift, hound him down!
                            [GHOST *sinks.*]

FIRST FURY [*awaking*]
Up! rouse another as I rouse thee; up!
Sleep'st thou? Rise up, and spurning sleep away,
See we if false to us this prelude rang.

CHORUS OF FURIES
Alack, alack, O sisters, we have toiled,
    O much and vainly have we toiled and borne!
Vainly! and all we wrought the gods have foiled,

And turnèd us to scorn!
He hath slipped from the net, whom we chased: he hath 'scaped
    us who should be our prey —
O'ermastered by slumber we sank, and our quarry hath stolen
    away!
Thou, child of the high God Zeus, Apollo, hast robbed us and
    wronged;
Thou, a youth, hast down-trodden the right that to godship more
    ancient belonged;
Thou hast cherished thy suppliant man; the slayer, the God-
    forsaken,
The bane of a parent, by craft from out of our grasp thou hast
    taken;
A god, thou hast stolen from us the avengers a matricide son —
And who shall consider thy deed and say, *It is rightfully done?*
                The sound of chiding scorn
                Came from the land of dream;
        Deep to mine inmost heart I felt it thrill and burn,
            Thrust as a strong-grasped goad, to urge
                Onward the chariot's team.
            Thrilled, chilled with bitter inward pain
        I stand as one beneath the doomsman's scourge.
        Shame on the younger gods who tread down right,
                Sitting on thrones of might!
        Woe on the altar of earth's central fane!
                Clotted on step and shrine,
Behold, the guilt of blood, the ghastly stain!
    Woe upon thee, Apollo! uncontrolled,
        Unbidden, hast thou, prophet-god, imbrued
        The pure prophetic shrine with wrongful blood!
    For thou too heinous a respect didst hold
Of man, too little heed of powers divine!
        And us the Fates, the ancients of the earth,
                Didst deem as nothing worth.
Scornful to me thou art, yet shalt not fend
    My wrath from him; though unto hell he flee,
                There too are we!
And he the blood defiled, should feel and rue,
Though I were not, fiend-wrath that shall not end,
Descending on his head who foully slew.
                    [*Re-enter* APOLLO *from the inner shrine.*]

APOLLO
Out! I command you. Out from this my home —
Haste, tarry not! Out from the mystic shrine,
Lest thy lot be to take into thy breast
The winged bright dart that from my golden string
Speeds hissing as a snake, — lest, pierced and thrilled
With agony, thou shouldst spew forth again
Black frothy heart's-blood, drawn from mortal men,
Belching the gory clots sucked forth from wounds.
These be no halls where such as you can prowl —
Go where men lay on men the doom of blood,
Heads lopped from necks, eyes from their spheres plucked out,
Hacked flesh, the flower of youthful seed crushed out,
Feet hewn away, and hands, and death beneath
The smiting stone, low moans and piteous
Of men impaled — Hark, hear ye for what feast
Ye hanker ever, and the loathing gods
Do spit upon your craving? Lo, your shape
Is all too fitted to your greed; the cave
Where lurks some lion, lapping gore, were home
More meet for you. Avaunt from sacred shrines,
Nor bring pollution by your touch on all
That nears you. Hence! and roam unshepherded —
No god there is to tend such herd as you.

CHORUS
O king Apollo, in our turn hear us.
Thou hast not only part in these ill things,
But art chief cause and doer of the same.

APOLLO
How? stretch thy speech to tell this, and have done.

CHORUS
Thine oracle bade this man slay his mother.

APOLLO
I bade him quit his sire's death, — wherefore not?

CHORUS
>Then didst thou aid and guard red-handed crime.

APOLLO
>Yea, and I bade him to this temple flee.

CHORUS
>And yet forsooth dost chide us following him!

APOLLO
>Ay — not for you it is, to near this fane.

CHORUS
>Yet is such office ours, imposed by fate.

APOLLO
>What office? vaunt the thing ye deem so fair.

CHORUS
>From home to home we chase the matricide.

APOLLO
>What? to avenge a wife who slays her lord?

CHORUS
>That is not blood outpoured by kindred hands.

APOLLO
>How darkly ye dishonour and annul
>The troth to which the high accomplishers,
>Hera and Zeus, do honour. Yea, and thus
>Is Aphrodite to dishonour cast,
>The queen of rapture unto mortal men.
>Know, that above the marriage-bed ordained
>For man and woman standeth Right as guard,
>Enhancing sanctity of troth-plight sworn;

Therefore, if thou art placable to those
Who have their consort slain, nor will'st to turn
On them the eye of wrath, unjust art thou
In hounding to his doom the man who slew
His mother. Lo, I know thee full of wrath
Against one deed, but all too placable
Unto the other, minishing the crime.
But in this cause shall Pallas guard the right.

CHORUS

Deem not my quest shall ever quit that man.

APOLLO

Follow then, make thee double toil in vain!

CHORUS

Think not by speech mine office to curtail.

APOLLO

None hast thou, that I would accept of thee!

CHORUS

Yea, high thine honour by the throne of Zeus:
But I, drawn on by scent of mother's blood,
Seek vengeance on this man and hound him down.

APOLLO

But I will stand beside him; 'tis for me
To guard my suppliant: gods and men alike
Do dread the curse of such an one betrayed,
And in me Fear and Will say *Leave him not.*   [*Exeunt omnes.*]

> *The scene changes to Athens. In the foreground, the*
> *Temple of Athena on the Acropolis; her statue stands*
> *in the centre;* ORESTES *is seen clinging to it.*

ORESTES

Look on me, queen Athena; lo, I come
By Loxias' behest; thou of thy grace

Receive me, driven of avenging powers —
Not now a red-hand slayer unannealed,
But with guilt fading, half-effaced, outworn
On many homes and paths of mortal men.
For to the limit of each land, each sea,
I roamed, obedient to Apollo's hest,
And come at last, O Goddess, to thy fane,
And clinging to thine image, bide my doom.

[*Enter the* CHORUS OF FURIES, *questing like hounds.*]

CHORUS

Ho! clear is here the trace of him we seek:
Follow the track of blood, the silent sign!
Like to some hound that hunts a wounded fawn,
We snuff along the scent of dripping gore,
And inwardly we pant, for many a day
Toiling in chase that shall fordo the man;
For o'er and o'er the wide land have I ranged,
And o'er the wide sea, flying without wings,
Swift as a sail I pressed upon his track,
Who now hard by is crouching, well I wot,
For scent of mortal blood allures me here.

Follow, seek him — round and round
Scent and snuff and scan the ground,
Lest unharmed he slip away,
He who did his mother slay!
Hist — he is there! See him his arms entwine
Around the image of the maid divine —
Thus aided, for the deed he wrought
Unto the judgment wills he to be brought.

It may not be! a mother's blood, poured forth
Upon the stainèd earth,
None gathers up: it lies — bear witness, Hell! —
For aye indelible!
And thou who sheddest it shalt give thine own
That shedding to atone!
Yea, from thy living limbs I suck it out,
Red, clotted, gout by gout, —
A draught abhorred of men and gods; but I
Will drain it, suck thee dry;

Yea, I will waste thee living, nerve and vein;
    Yea, for thy mother slain,
Will drag thee downward, there where thou shalt dree
    The weird of agony!
And thou and whatsoe'er of men hath sinned —
    Hath wronged or God, or friend,
Or parent, — learn ye how to all and each
    The arm of doom can reach!
Sternly requiteth, in the world beneath,
    The judgment-seat of Death;
Yea, Death, beholding every man's endeavour,
    Recordeth it for ever.

ORESTES
    I, schooled in many miseries, have learnt
    How many refuges of cleansing shrines
    There be; I know when law alloweth speech
    And when imposeth silence. Lo, I stand
    Fixed now to speak, for he whose word is wise
    Commands the same. Look, how the stain of blood
    Is dull upon mine hand and wastes away,
    And laved and lost therewith is the deep curse
    Of matricide; for while the guilt was new,
    'Twas banished from me at Apollo's hearth,
    Atoned and purified by death of swine.
    Long were my word if I should sum the tale,
    How oft since then among my fellow-men
    I stood and brought no curse. Time cleanses all —
    Time, the coeval of all things that are.
    Now from pure lips, in words of omen fair,
    I call Athena, lady of this land,
    To come, my champion: so, in aftertime,
    She shall not fail of love and service leal,
    Not won by war, from me and from my land
    And all the folk of Argos, vowed to her.
      Now, be she far away in Libyan land
    Where flows from Triton's lake her natal wave, —
    Stand she with planted feet, or in some hour
    Of rest conceal them, champion of her friends
    Where'er she be, — or whether o'er the plain
    Phlegraean she look forth, as warrior bold —

I cry to her to come, where'er she be,
(And she, as goddess, from afar can hear,)
And aid and free me, set among my foes.

CHORUS
Thee not Apollo nor Athena's strength
Can save from perishing, a castaway
Amid the Lost, where no delight shall meet
Thy soul — a bloodless prey of nether powers,
A shadow among shadows. Answerest thou
Nothing? dost cast away my words with scorn,
Thou, prey prepared and dedicate to me?
Not as a victim slain upon the shrine,
But living shalt thou see thy flesh my food.
Hear now the binding chant that makes thee mine.

Weave the weird dance, — behold the hour
    To utter forth the chant of hell,
    Our sway among mankind to tell,
The guidance of our power.
Of Justice are we ministers,
    And whosoe'er of men may stand
    Lifting a pure unsullied hand,
That man no doom of ours incurs,
    And walks thro' all his mortal path
    Untouched by woe, unharmed by wrath.
    But if, as yonder man, he hath
Blood on the hands he strives to hide,
    We stand avengers at his side,
Decreeing, *Thou hast wronged the dead*:
    We are doom's witnesses to thee.
The price of blood, his hands have shed,
We wring from him; in life, in death,
    Hard at his side are we!

Night, Mother Night, who brought me forth, a torment
        To living men and dead,
Hear me, O hear! by Leto's stripling son
        I am dishonourèd:
He hath ta'en from me him who cowers in refuge,
        To me made consecrate, —

A rightful victim, him who slew his mother.
  Given o'er to me and fate.

    Hear the hymn of hell,
      O'er the victim sounding, —
    Chant of frenzy, chant of ill,
      Sense and will confounding!
    Round the soul entwining
      Without lute or lyre —
    Soul in madness pining,
      Wasting as with fire!

Fate, all-pervading Fate, this service spun, commanding
  That I should bide therein:
Whosoe'er of mortals, made perverse and lawless,
  Is stained with blood of kin,
By his side are we, and hunt him ever onward,
  Till to the Silent Land,
The realm of death, he cometh; neither yonder
  In freedom shall he stand.

    Hear the hymn of hell,
      O'er the victim sounding, —
    Chant of frenzy, chant of ill,
      Sense and will confounding!
    Round the soul entwining
      Without lute or lyre —
    Soul in madness pining,
      Wasting as with fire!

When from womb of Night we sprang, on us this labour
  Was laid and shall abide.
Gods immortal are ye, yet beware ye touch not
  That which is our pride!
None may come beside us gathered round the blood feast —
  For us no garments white
Gleam on a festal day; for us a darker fate is,
  Another darker rite.
That is mine hour when falls an ancient line —
  When in the household's heart

The god of blood doth slay by kindred hands, —
          Then do we bear our part:
On him who slays we sweep with chasing cry:
          Though he be triply strong,
We wear and waste him; blood atones for blood,
          New pain for ancient wrong.

I hold this task — 'tis mine, and not another's.
          The very gods on high,
Though they can silence and annul the prayers
          Of those who on us cry,
They may not strive with us who stand apart,
          A race by Zeus abhorred,
Blood-boltered, held unworthy of the council
          And converse of Heaven's lord.
Therefore the more I leap upon my prey;
          Upon their head I bound;
My foot is hard; as one that trips a runner
          I cast them to the ground;
Yea, to the depth of doom intolerable;
          And they who erst were great,
And upon earth held high their pride and glory,
          Are brought to low estate.
In underworld they waste and are diminished,
          The while around them fleet
Dark wavings of my robes, and, subtly woven,
          The paces of my feet.

Who falls infatuate, he sees not, neither knows he
          That we are at his side;
So closely round about him, darkly flitting,
          The cloud of guilt doth glide.
Heavily 'tis uttered, how around his hearthstone
          The mirk of hell doth rise.
Stern and fixed the law is; we have hands t' achieve it,
          Cunning to devise.
Queens are we and mindful of our solemn vengeance.
          Not by tear or prayer
Shall a man avert it. In unhonoured darkness,
          Far from gods, we fare,

Lit unto our task with torch of sunless regions,
     And o'er a deadly way —
Deadly to the living as to those who see not
     Life and light of day —
Hunt we and press onward. Who of mortals hearing
     Doth not quake for awe,
Hearing all that Fate thro' hand of God hath given us
     For ordinance and law?
Yea, this right to us, in dark abysm and backward
     Of ages it befel:
None shall wrong mine office, tho' in nether regions
     And sunless dark I dwell.
                [*Enter* ATHENA *from above.*]

ATHENA
    Far off I heard the clamour of your cry,
    As by Scamander's side I set my foot
    Asserting right upon the land given o'er
    To me by those who o'er Achaia's host
    Held sway and leadership: no scanty part
    Of all they won by spear and sword, to me
    They gave it, land and all that grew theron,
    As chosen heirloom for my Theseus' clan.
    Thence summoned, sped I with a tireless foot, —
    Hummed on the wind, instead of wings, the fold
    Of this mine aegis, by my feet propelled,
    As, linked to mettled horses, speeds a car.
    And now, beholding here Earth's nether brood,
    I fear it nought, yet are mine eyes amazed
    With wonder. Who are ye? of all I ask,
    And of this stranger to my statue clinging.
    But ye — your shape is like no human form,
    Like to no goddess whom the gods behold,
    Like to no shape which mortal women wear.
    Yet to stand by and chide a monstrous form
    Is all unjust — from such words Right revolts.

CHORUS
    O child of Zeus, one word shall tell thee all.
    We are the children of eternal Night,
    And Furies in the underworld are called.

ATHENA
>I know your lineage now and eke your name.

CHORUS
>Yea, and eftsoons indeed my rights shalt know.

ATHENA
>Fain would I learn them; speak them clearly forth.

CHORUS
>We chase from home the murderers of men.

ATHENA
>And where at last can he that slew make pause?

CHORUS
>Where this is law — *All joy abandon here.*

ATHENA
>Say, do ye bay this man to such a flight?

CHORUS
>Yea, for of choice he did his mother slay.

ATHENA
>Urged by no fear of other wrath and doom?

CHORUS
>What spur can rightly goad to matricide?

ATHENA
>Two stand to plead — one only have I heard.

CHORUS
> He will not swear nor challenge us to oath.

ATHENA
> The form of justice, not its deed, thou willest.

CHORUS
> Prove thou that word; thou art not scant of skill.

ATHENA
> I say that oaths shall not enforce the wrong.

CHORUS
> Then test the cause, judge and award the right.

ATHENA
> Will ye to me then this decision trust?

CHORUS
> Yea, reverencing true child of worthy sire.

ATHENA [To ORESTES)
> O man unknown, make thou thy plea in turn.
> Speak forth thy land, thy lineage, and thy woes;
> Then, if thou canst, avert this bitter blame —
> If, as I deem, in confidence of right
> Thou sittest hard beside my holy place,
> Clasping this statue, as Ixion sat,
> A sacred suppliant for Zeus to cleanse, —
> To all this answer me in words made plain.

ORESTES
> O queen Athena, first from thy last words
> Will I a great solicitude remove.
> Not one blood-guilty am I; no foul stain
> Clings to thine image from my clinging hand;

Whereof one potent proof I have to tell.
Lo, the law stands — *The slayer shall not plead,*
Till by the hand of him who cleanses blood
A suckling creature's blood besprinkle him.
Long since have I this expiation done, —
In many a home, slain beasts and running streams
Have cleansed me. Thus I speak away that fear.
Next, of my lineage quickly thou shalt learn:
An Argive am I, and right well thou know'st
My sire, that Agamemnon who arrayed
The fleet and them that went therein to war —
That chief with whom thy hand combined to crush
To an uncitied heap what once was Troy;
That Agamemnon, when he homeward came,
Was brought unto no honourable death,
Slain by the dark-souled wife who brought me forth
To him, — enwound and slain in wily nets,
Blazoned with blood that in the laver ran.
And I, returning from an exiled youth,
Slew her, my mother — lo, it stands avowed!
With blood for blood avenging my loved sire;
And in this deed doth Loxias bear part,
Decreeing agonies, to goad my will,
Unless by me the guilty found their doom.
Do thou decide if right or wrong were done —
Thy dooming, whatsoe'er it be, contents me.

ATHENA

Too mighty is this matter, whatsoe'er
Of mortals claims to judge hereof aright.
Yea, me, even me, eternal Right forbids
To judge the issues of blood-guilt, and wrath
That follows swift behind. This too gives pause,
That thou as one with all due rites performed
Dost come, unsinning, pure, unto my shrine.
Whate'er thou art, in this my city's name,
As uncondemned, I take thee to my side, —
Yet have these foes of thine such dues by fate,
I may not banish them: and if they fail,
O'erthrown in judgment of the cause, forthwith
Their anger's poison shall infect the land —

A dropping plague-spot of eternal ill.
Thus stand we with a woe on either hand:
Stay they, or go at my commandment forth,
Perplexity or pain must needs befall.
Yet, as on me Fate hath imposed the cause,
I choose unto me judges that shall be
An ordinance for ever, set to rule
The dues of blood-guilt, upon oath declared.
But ye, call forth your witness and your proof,
Words strong for justice, fortified by oath;
And I, whoe'er are truest in my town,
Them will I chose and bring, and straitly charge,
Look on this cause, discriminating well,
And pledge your oath to utter nought of wrong. [*Exit* ATHENA.]

CHORUS
Now are they all undone, the ancient laws,
     If here the slayer's cause
Prevail; new wrong for ancient right shall be
     If matricide go free.
Henceforth a deed like his by all shall stand,
     Too ready to the hand:
Too oft shall parents in the aftertime
     Rue and lament this crime, —
Taught, not in false imagining, to feel
     Their children's thrusting steel:
No more the wrath, that erst on murder fell
     From us, the queens of Hell,
Shall fall, no more our watching gaze impend —
     Death shall smite unrestrained.

Henceforth shall one unto another cry
Lo, they are stricken, lo, they fall and die
Around me! and that other answers him,
O thou that lookest that thy woes should cease,
     Behold, with dark increase
They throng and press upon thee; yea, and dim
     Is all the cure, and every comfort vain!

Let none henceforth cry out, when falls the blow
     Of sudden-smiting woe,

Cry out in sad reiterated strain
O Justice, aid! aid, O ye thrones of Hell!
     So though a father or a mother wail
New-smitten by a son, it shall no more avail,
Since, overthrown by wrong, the fane of Justice fell!

Know, that a throne there is that may not pass away,
     And one that sitteth on it — even Fear,
Searching with steadfast eyes man's inner soul:
Wisdom is child of pain, and born with many a tear;
          But who henceforth,
What man of mortal men, what nation upon earth,
     That holdeth nought in awe nor in the light
     Of inner reverence, shall worship Right
          As in the older day?

Praise not, O man, the life beyond control,
Nor that which bows unto a tyrant's sway.
          Know that the middle way
Is dearest unto God, and they thereon who wend,
          They shall achieve the end;
     But they who wander or to left or right
          Are sinners in his sight.
     Take to thy heart this one, this soothfast word —
          Of wantonness impiety is sire;
     Only from calm control and sanity unstirred
Cometh true weal, the goal of every man's desire.

Yea, whatsoe'er befall, hold thou this word of mine:
          Bow down at Justice' shrine,
     Turn thou thine eyes away from earthly lure,
     Nor with a godless foot that altar spurn.
     For as thou dost shall Fate do in return,
          And the great doom is sure.
     Therefore let each adore a parent's trust,
          And each with loyalty revere the guest
               That in his halls doth rest.
For whoso uncompelled doth follow what is just,
          He ne'er shall be unblest;
     Yea, never to the gulf of doom
          That man shall come.

But he whose will is set against the gods,
  Who treads beyond the law with foot impure,
Till o'er the wreck of Right confusion broods, —
  Know that for him, though now he sail secure,
The day of storm shall be; then shall he strive and fail
Down from the shivered yard to furl the sail,
And call on Powers, that heed him nought, to save,
  And vainly wrestle with the whirling wave.
        Hot was his heart with pride —
        I shall not fall, he cried.
        But him with watching scorn
        The god beholds, forlorn,
  Tangled in toils of Fate beyond escape,
  Hopeless of haven safe beyond the cape —
Till all his wealth and bliss of bygone day
  Upon the reef of Rightful Doom is hurled,
        And he is rapt away
Unwept, for ever, to the dead forgotten world.
        [*Re-enter* ATHENA, *with twelve Athenian Citizens.*]

ATHENA
  O herald, make proclaim, bid all men come.
  Then let the shrill blast of the Tyrrhene trump,
  Fulfilled with mortal breath, thro' the wide air
  Peal a loud summons, bidding all men heed.
  For, till my judges fill this judgment-seat,
  Silence behoves, — that this whole city learn,
  What for all time mine ordinance commands,
  And these men, that the cause be judged aright.
        [APOLLO *approaches.*]

CHORUS
  O king Apollo, rule what is thine own,
  But in this thing what share pertains to thee?

APOLLO
  First, as a witness come I, for this man
  Is suppliant of mine by sacred right,
  Guest of my holy hearth and cleansed by me
  Of blood-guilt: then, to set me at his side

And in his cause bear part, as part I bore
Erst in his deed, whereby his mother fell.
Let whoso knoweth now announce the cause.

ATHENA [*To the* CHORUS]
    'Tis I announce the cause — first speech be yours;
    For rightfully shall they whose plaint is tried
    Tell the tale first and set the matter clear.

CHORUS
    Though we be many, brief shall be our tale.
    [*To* ORESTES] Answer thou, setting word to match with word;
    And first avow — hast thou thy mother slain?

ORESTES
    I slew her. I deny no word hereof.

CHORUS
    Three falls decide the wrestle — this is one.

ORESTES
    Thou vauntest thee — but o'er no final fall.

CHORUS
    Yet must thou tell the manner of thy deed.

ORESTES
    Drawn sword in hand, I gashed her neck. 'Tis told.

CHORUS
    But by whose word, whose craft, wert thou impelled?

ORESTES
    By oracles of him who here attests me.

CHORUS
    The prophet-god bade thee thy mother slay?

ORESTES
Yea, and thro' him less ill I fared, till now.

CHORUS
If the vote grip thee, thou shalt change that word.

ORESTES
Strong is my hope; my buried sire shall aid.

CHORUS
Go to now, trust the dead, a matricide!

ORESTES
Yea, for in her combined two stains of sin.

CHORUS
How? speak this clearly to the judges' mind.

ORESTES
Slaying her husband, she did slay my sire.

CHORUS
Therefore thou livest; death assoils her deed.

ORESTES
Then while she lived why didst thou hunt her not?

CHORUS
She was not kin by blood to him she slew.

ORESTES
And I, am I by blood my mother's kin?

CHORUS

    O cursed with murder's guilt, how else wert thou
    The burden of her womb? Dost thou forswear
    Thy mother's kinship, closest bond of love?

ORESTES

    It is thine hour, Apollo — speak the law,
    Averring if this deed were justly done;
    For done it is, and clear and undenied.
    But if to thee this murder's cause seem right
    Or wrongful, speak — that I to these may tell.

APOLLO

    To you, Athena's mighty council-court,
    Justly for justice will I plead, even I,
    The prophet-god, nor cheat you by one word.
    For never spake I from my prophet-seat
    One word, of man, of woman, or of state,
    Save what the Father of Olympian gods
    Commanded unto me. I rede you then,
    Bethink you of my plea, how strong it stands,
    And follow the decree of Zeus our sire, —
    For oaths prevail not over Zeus' command.

CHORUS

    Go to; thou sayest that from Zeus befel
    The oracle that this Orestes bade
    With vengeance quit the slaying of his sire,
    And hold as nought his mother's right of kin!

APOLLO

    Yea, for it stands not with a common death,
    That he should die, a chieftain and a king
    Decked with the sceptre which high heaven confers —
    Die, and by female hands, not smitten down
    By a far-shooting bow, held stalwartly
    By some strong Amazon. Another doom
    Was his: O Pallas, hear, and ye who sit
    In judgment, to discern this thing aright! —
    She with a specious voice of welcome true

Hailed him, returning from the mighty mart
Where war for life gives fame, triumphant home;
Then o'er the laver, as he bathed himself,
She spread from head to foot a covering net,
And in the endless mesh of cunning robes
Enwound and trapped her lord, and smote him down.
Lo, ye have heard what doom this chieftain met,
The majesty of Greece, the fleet's high lord:
Such as I tell it, let it gall your ears,
Who stand as judges to decide this cause.

CHORUS

Zeus, as thou sayest, holds a father's death
As first of crimes, — yet he of his own act
Cast into chains his father, Cronos old:
How suits that deed with that which now ye tell?
O ye who judge, I bid ye mark my words!

APOLLO

O monsters loathed of all, O scorn of gods,
He that hath bound may loose: a cure there is,
Yea, many a plan that can unbind the chain.
But when the thirsty dust sucks up man's blood
Once shed in death, he shall arise no more.
No chant nor charm for this my Sire hath wrought.
All else there is, he moulds and shifts at will,
Not scant of strength nor breath, whate'er he do.

CHORUS

Think yet, for what acquittal thou dost plead:
He who hath shed a mother's kindred blood,
Shall he in Argos dwell, where dwelt his sire?
How shall he stand before the city's shrines,
How share the clansmen's holy lustral bowl?

APOLLO

This too I answer; mark a soothfast word,
Not the true parent is the woman's womb
That bears the child; she doth but nurse the seed

New-sown: the male is parent; she for him,
As stranger for a stranger, hoards the germ
Of life, unless the god its promise blight.
And proof hereof before you will I set.
Birth may from fathers, without mothers, be:
See at your side a witness of the same,
Athena, daughter of Olympian Zeus,
Never within the darkness of the womb
Fostered nor fashioned, but a bud more bright
Than any goddess in her breast might bear.
And I, O Pallas, howsoe'er I may,
Henceforth will glorify thy town, thy clan,
And for this end have sent my suppliant here
Unto thy shrine; that he from this time forth
Be loyal unto thee for evermore,
O goddess-queen, and thou unto thy side
Mayst win and hold him faithful, and his line,
And that for aye this pledge and troth remain
To children's children of Athenian seed.

ATHENA
    Enough is said; I bid the judges now
    With pure intent deliver just award.

CHORUS
    We too have shot our every shaft of speech,
    And now abide to hear the doom of law.

ATHENA [*To* APOLLO *and* ORESTES]
    Say, how ordaining shall I 'scape your blame?

APOLLO
    I spake, ye heard; enough. O stranger men,
    Heed well your oath as ye decide the cause.

ATHENA
    O men of Athens, ye who first do judge
    The law of bloodshed, hear me now ordain.
    Here to all time for Aegeus' Attic host

Shall stand this council-court of judges sworn,
Here the tribunal, set on Ares' Hill
Where camped of old the tented Amazons,
What time in hate of Theseus they assailed
Athens, and set against her citadel
A counterwork of new sky-pointing towers,
And there to Ares held their sacrifice,
Where now the rock hath name, even Ares' Hill.
And hence shall Reverence and her kinsman Fear
Pass to each free man's heart, by day and night
Enjoining, *Thou shalt do no unjust thing,*
So long as law stands as it stood of old
Unmarred by civic change. Look you, the spring
Is pure; but foul it once with influx vile
And muddy clay, and none can drink thereof.
Therefore, O citizens, I bid ye bow
In awe to this command, *Let no man live
Uncurbed by law nor curbed by tyranny;*
Nor banish ye the monarchy of Awe
Beyond the walls; untouched by fear divine,
No man doth justice in the world of men.
Therefore in purity and holy dread
Stand and revere; so shall ye have and hold
A saving bulwark of the state and land,
Such as no man hath ever elsewhere known,
Nor in far Scythia, nor in Pelops' realm.
Thus I ordain it now, a council-court
Pure and unsullied by the lust of gain,
Sacred and swift to vengeance, wakeful ever
To champion men who sleep, the country's guard.
Thus have I spoken, thus to mine own clan
Commended it for ever. Ye who judge,
Arise, take each his vote, mete out the right,
Your oath revering. Lo, my word is said.

>   [*The twelve come forward, one by one, to the urns of
>   decision; the first votes; as each of the others follows,
>   the* CHORUS *and* APOLLO *speak alternately.*]

CHORUS
I rede ye well, beware! nor put to shame,
In aught, this grievous company of hell.

APOLLO
>I too would warn you, fear mine oracles —
>From Zeus they are, — nor make them void of fruit.

CHORUS
>Presumptuous is thy claim, blood-guilt to judge,
>And false henceforth thine oracles shall be.

APOLLO
>Failed then the counsels of my sire, when turned
>Ixion, first of slayers, to his side?

CHORUS
>These are but words; but I, if justice fail me,
>Will haunt this land in grim and deadly deed.

APOLLO
>Scorn of the younger and the elder gods
>Art thou: 'tis I that shall prevail anon.

CHORUS
>Thus didst thou too of old in Pheres' halls,
>O'erreaching Fate to make a mortal deathless.

APOLLO
>Was it not well, my worshipper to aid,
>Then most of all when hardest was the need?

CHORUS
>I say thou didst annul the lots of life,
>Cheating with wine the deities of eld.

APOLLO
>I say thou shalt anon, thy pleadings foiled,
>Spit venom vainly on thine enemies.

CHORUS

    Since this young god o'errides mine ancient right,
    I tarry but to claim your law, not knowing
    If wrath of mine shall blast your state or spare.

ATHENA

    Mine is the right to add the final vote,
    And I award it to Orestes' cause.
    For me no mother bore within her womb,
    And, save for wedlock evermore eschewed,
    I vouch myself the champion of the man,
    Not of the woman, yea, with all my soul, —
    In heart, as birth, a father's child alone.
    Thus will I not too heinously regard
    A woman's death who did her husband slay,
    The guardian of her home; and if the votes
    Equal do fall, Orestes shall prevail.
    Ye of the judges who are named thereto,
    Swiftly shake forth the lots from either urn.
                        [Two judges come forward, one to each urn.]

ORESTES

    O bright Apollo, what shall be the end?

CHORUS

    O Night, dark mother mine, dost mark these things?

ORESTES

    Now shall my doom be life, or strangling cords.

CHORUS

    And mine, lost honour or a wider sway.

APOLLO

    O stranger judges, sum aright the count
    Of votes cast forth, and, parting them, take heed
    Ye err not in decision. The default
    Of one vote only bringeth ruin deep,
    One, cast aright, doth stablish house and home.

ATHENA

> Behold, this man is free from guilt of blood,
> For half the votes condemn him, half set free!

ORESTES

> O Pallas, light and safety of my home,
> Thou, thou hast given me back to dwell once more
> In that my fatherland, amerced of which
> I wandered; now shall Grecian lips say this,
> *The man is Argive once again, and dwells*
> *Again within his father's wealthy hall,*
> *By Pallas saved, by Loxias, and by Him,*
> *The great third saviour, Zeus omnipotent —*
> Who thus in pity for my father's fate
> Doth pluck me from my doom, beholding these,
> Confederates of my mother. Lo, I pass
> To mine own home, but proffering this vow
> Unto thy land and people: *Nevermore,*
> *Thro' all the manifold years of Time to be,*
> *Shall any chieftain of mine Argive land*
> *Bear hitherward his spears for fight arrayed.*
> For we, though lapped in earth we then shall lie,
> By thwart adversities will work our will
> On them who shall transgress this oath of mine,
> Paths of despair and journeyings ill-starred
> For them ordaining, till their task they rue.
> But if this oath be rightly kept, to them
> Will we the dead be full of grace, the while
> With loyal league they honour Pallas' town.
> And now farewell, thou and thy city's folk —
> Firm be thine arm's grasp, closing with thy foes,
> And, strong to save, bring victory to thy spear.
>
> > [*Exit* ORESTES, *with* APOLLO.]

CHORUS

> Woe on you, younger gods! the ancient right
> Ye have o'erridden, rent it from my hands.
>
> I am dishonoured of you, thrust to scorn!
> > But heavily my wrath

Shall on this land fling forth the drops that blast and burn.
   Venom of vengeance, that shall work such scathe
   As I have suffered; where that dew shall fall,
      Shall leafless blight arise,
   Wasting Earth's offspring, — Justice, hear my call! —
   And thorough all the land in deadly wise
   Shall scatter venom, to exude again
      In pestilence on men.
   What cry avails me now, what deed of blood,
   Unto this land what dark despite?
      Alack, alack, forlorn
   Are we, a bitter injury have borne!
   Alack, O sisters, O dishonoured brood
      Of mother Night!

ATHENA
   Nay, bow ye to my words, chafe not nor moan:
   Ye are not worsted nor disgraced; behold,
   With balanced vote the cause had issue fair,
   Nor in the end did aught dishonour thee.
   But thus the will of Zeus shone clearly forth,
   And his own prophet-god avouched the same,
   Orestes slew: his slaying is atoned.
   Therefore I pray you, not upon this land
   Shoot forth the dart of vengeance; be appeased,
   Nor blast the land with blight, nor loose thereon
   Drops of eternal venom, direful darts
   Wasting and marring nature's seed of growth.
   For I, the queen of Athens' sacred right,
   Do pledge to you a holy sanctuary
   Deep in the heart of this my land, made just
   By your indwelling presence, while ye sit
   Hard by your sacred shrines that gleam with oil
   Of sacrifice, and by this folk adored.

CHORUS
   Woe on you, younger gods! the ancient right
   Ye have o'erridden, rent it from my hands.

   I am dishonoured of you, thrust to scorn!
      But heavily my wrath

Shall on his land fling forth the drops that blast and burn.
Venom of vengeance, that shall work such scathe
As I have suffered; where that dew shall fall,
Shall leafless blight arise,
Wasting Earth's offspring, — Justice, hear my call! —
And thorough all the land in deadly wise
Shall scatter venom, to exude again
In pestilence of men.
What cry avails me now, what deed of blood,
Unto this land what dark despite?
Alack, alack, forlorn
Are we, a bitter injury have borne!
Alack, O sisters, O dishonoured brood
Of mother Night!

ATHENA

Dishonoured are ye not; turn not, I pray,
As goddesses your swelling wrath on men,
Nor make the friendly earth despiteful to them.
I too have Zeus for champion — 'tis enough —
I only of all goddesses do know.
To ope the chamber where his thunderbolts
Lie stored and sealed; but here is no such need.
Nay, be appeased, nor cast upon the ground
The malice of thy tongue, to blast the world;
Calm thou thy bitter wrath's black inward surge,
For high shall be thine honour, set beside me
For ever in this land, whose fertile lap
Shall pour its teeming firstfruits unto you,
Gifts for fair childbirth and for wedlock's crown:
Thus honoured, praise my spoken pledge for aye.

CHORUS

I, I dishonoured in this earth to dwell, —
Ancient of days and wisdom! I breathe forth
Poison and breath of frenzied ire. O Earth,
Woe, woe, for thee, for me!
From side to side what pains be these that thrill?
Hearken, O mother Night, my wrath, mine agony!

Whom from mine ancient rights the gods have thrust,
      And brought me to the dust —
Woe, woe is me! — with craft invincible.

ATHENA

    Older art thou than I, and I will bear
    With this thy fury. Know, although thou be
    More wise in ancient wisdom, yet have I
    From Zeus no scanted measure of the same,
    Wherefore take heed unto this prophecy —
    If to another land of alien men
    Ye go, too late shall ye feel longing deep
    For mine. The rolling tides of time bring round
    A day of brighter glory for this town;
    And thou, enshrined in honour by the halls
    Where dwelt Erechtheus, shalt a worship win
    From men and from the train of womankind,
    Greater than any tribe elsewhere shall pay.
    Cast thou not therefore on this soil of mine
    Whetstones that sharpen souls to bloodshedding,
    The burning goads of youthful hearts, made hot
    With frenzy of the spirit, not of wine.
    Nor pluck as 'twere the heart from cocks that strive,
    To set it in the breasts of citizens
    Of mine, a war-god's spirit, keen for fight,
    Made stern against their country and their kin.
    The man who grievously doth lust for fame,
    War, full, immitigable, let him wage
    Against the stranger; but of kindred birds
    I hold the challenge hateful. Such the boon
    I proffer thee — within this land of lands,
    Most loved of gods, with me to show and share
    Fair mercy, gratitude and grace as fair.

CHORUS

    I, I dishonoured in this earth to dwell, —
    Ancient of days and wisdom! I breathe forth
    Poison and breath of frenzied ire. O Earth,
          Woe, woe, for thee, for me!
    From side to side what pains be these that thrill?

' Hearken, O mother Night, my wrath, mine agony!
Whom from mine ancient rights the gods have thrust,
　　　　And brought me to the dust —
Woe, woe is me! — with craft invincible.

ATHENA
　　I will not weary of soft words to thee,
　　That never mayst thou say, *Behold me spurned,*
　　An elder by a younger deity,
　　And from this land rejected and forlorn,
　　Unhonoured by the men who dwell therein.
　　But, if Persuasion's grace be sacred to thee,
　　Soft in the soothing accents of my tongue,
　　Tarry, I pray thee; yet, if go thou wilt,
　　Not rightfully wilt thou on this my town
　　Sway down the scale that beareth wrath and teen
　　Or wasting plague upon this folk. 'Tis thine,
　　If so thou wilt, inheritress to be
　　Of this my land, its utmost grace to win.

CHORUS
　　O queen, what refuge dost thou promise me?

ATHENA
　　Refuge untouched by bale: take thou my boon.

CHORUS
　　What, if I take it, shall mine honour be?

ATHENA
　　No house shall prosper without grace of thine.

CHORUS
　　Canst thou achieve and grant such power to me?

ATHENA
　　Yea, for my hand shall bless thy worshippers.

CHORUS
　　And wilt thou pledge me this for time eterne?

ATHENA
> Yea: none can bid me pledge beyond my power.

CHORUS
> Lo, I desist from wrath, appeased by thee.

ATHENA
> Then in the land's heart shalt thou win thee friends.

CHORUS
> What chant dost bid me raise, to greet the land?

ATHENA
> Such as aspires towards a victory
> Unrued by any: chants from breast of earth,
> From wave, from sky; and let the wild winds' breath
> Pass with soft sunlight o'er the lap of land, —
> Strong wax the fruits of earth, fair teem the kine,
> Unfailing, for my town's prosperity,
> And constant be the growth of mortal seed.
> But more and more root out the impious,
> For as a gardener fosters what he sows,
> So foster I this race, whom righteousness
> Doth fend from sorrow. Such the proffered boon.
> But I, if wars must be, and their loud clash
> And carnage, for my town, will ne'er endure
> That aught but victory shall crown her fame.

CHORUS
> Lo, I accept it; at her very side
>   Doth Pallas bid me dwell:
> I will not wrong the city of her pride,
> Which even Almighty Zeus and Ares hold
>   Heaven's earthly citadel,
> Loved home of Grecian gods, the young, the old,
>   The sanctuary divine,
>   The shield of every shrine!

For Athens I say forth a gracious prophecy, —
The glory of the sunlight and the skies
Shall bid from earth arise
Warm wavelets of new life and glad prosperity.

ATHENA

Behold, with gracious heart well pleased
I for my citizens do grant
Fulfilment of this covenant:
And here, their wrath at length appeased,
These mighty deities shall stay,
For theirs it is by right to sway
The lot that rules our mortal day,
And he who hath not inly felt
Their stern decree, ere long on him,
Not knowing why and whence, the grim
Life-crushing blow is dealt.
The father's sin upon the child
Descends, and sin is silent death,
And leads him on the downward path,
By stealth beguiled,
Unto the Furies: though his state
On earth were high, and loud his boast,
Victim of silent ire and hate
He dwells among the Lost.

CHORUS

To my blessing now give ear. —
Scorching blight nor singèd air
Never blast thine olives fair!
Drouth, that wasteth bud and plant,
Keep to thine own place. Avaunt,
Famine fell, and come not hither
Stealthily to waste and wither!
Let the land, in season due,
Twice her waxing fruits renew;
Teem the kine in double measure;
Rich in new god-given treasure;
Here let men the powers adore
For sudden gifts unhoped before!

ATHENA

> O hearken, warders of the wall
> That guards mine Athens, what a dower
> Is unto her ordained and given!
> For mighty is the Furies' power,
> And deep-revered in courts of heaven
> And realms of hell; and clear to all
> They weave thy doom, mortality!
> And some in joy and peace shall sing;
> But unto other some they bring
> Sad life and tear-dimmed eye.

CHORUS

> And far away I ban thee and remove,
> Untimely death of youths too soon brought low!
> And to each maid, O gods, when time is come for love,
> Grant ye a warrior's heart, a wedded life to know.
> Ye too, O Fates, children of mother Night,
> Whose children too are we, O goddesses
> Of just award, of all by sacred right
> Queens who in time and in eternity
> Do rule, a present power for righteousness,
> Honoured beyond all Gods, hear ye and grant my cry!

ATHENA

> And I too, I with joy am fain,
> Hearing your voice this gift ordain
> Unto my land. High thanks be thine,
> Persuasion, who with eyes divine
> Into my tongue didst look thy strength,
> To bend and to appease at length
> Those who would not be comforted.
> Zeus, king of parley, doth prevail,
> And ye and I will strive nor fail,
> That good may stand in evil's stead,
> And lasting bliss for bale.

CHORUS

> And nevermore these walls within
> Shall echo fierce sedition's din
> Unslaked with blood and crime;

The thirsty dust shall nevermore
Suck up the darkly streaming gore
Of civic broils, shed out in wrath
And vengeance, crying death for death!
But man with man and state with state
Shall vow *The pledge of common hate*
And common friendship, that for man
Hath oft made blessing out of ban,
   Be ours unto all time.

ATHENA

Skill they, or not, the path to find
Of favouring speech and presage kind?
Yea, even from these, who, grim and stern,
   Glared anger upon you of old,
O citizens, ye now shall earn
   A recompense right manifold.
Deck them aright, extol them high,
Be loyal to their loyalty,
   And ye shall make your town and land
   Sure, propped on Justice' saving hand,
      And Fame's eternity.

CHORUS

Hail ye, all hail! and yet again, all hail,
   O Athens, happy in a weal secured!
O ye who sit by Zeus' right hand, nor fail
   Of wisdom set among you and assured,
Loved of the well-loved Goddess-Maid! the King
Of gods doth reverence you, beneath her guarding wing.

ATHENA

All hail unto each honoured guest!
Whom to the chambers of your rest
'Tis mine to lead, and to provide
The hallowed torch, the guard and guide.
Pass down, the while these altars glow
With sacred fire, to earth below
   And your appointed shrine.

There dwelling, from the land restrain
The force of fate, the breath of bane,
But waft on us the gift and gain
    Of Victory divine!
And ye, the men of Cranaos' seed,
I bid you now with reverence lead
These alien Powers that thus are made
Athenian evermore. To you
Fair be their will henceforth, to do
    Whate'er may bless and aid!

CHORUS

    Hail to you all! hail yet again,
All who love Athens, Gods and men,
    Adoring her as Pallas' home!
And while ye reverence what ye grant —
My sacred shrine and hidden haunt —
    Blameless and blissful be your doom!

ATHENA

Once more I praise the promise of your vows,
And now I bid the golden torches' glow
Pass down before you to the hidden depth
Of earth, by mine own sacred servants borne,
My loyal guards of statue and of shrine.
Come forth, O flower of Theseus' Attic land,
O glorious band of children and of wives,
And ye, O train of matrons crowned with eld!
Deck you with festal robes of scarlet dye
In honour of this day: O gleaming torch,
Lead onward, that these gracious powers of earth
Henceforth be seen to bless the life of men.
    [ATHENA *leads the procession downwards into the Cave of the*
    Furies, under Areopagus: as they go, the escort of women and
        children chant aloud.]

CHANT

With loyalty we lead you; proudly go,
Night's childless children, to your home below!
    (*O citizens, awhile from words forbear!*)
    To darkness' deep primeval lair,

Far in Earth's bosom, downward fare,
Adored with prayer and sacrifice.
　　(*O citizens, forbear your cries!*)
Pass hitherward, ye powers of Dread,
With all your former wrath allayed,
　　Into the heart of this loved land;
With joy unto your temple wend,
The while upon your steps attend
　　The flames that fed upon the brand —
(*Now, now ring out your chant, your joy's acclaim!*)
　　Behind them, as they downward fare,
　　Let holy hands libations bear,
　　　　And torches' sacred flame.
　　All-seeing Zeus and Fate come down
　　To battle fair for Pallas' town!
Ring out your chant, ring out your joy's acclaim!

　　　　　　　　　　　　　　　　[*Exeunt omnes.*]

　　　　　　The End